THE
REVIVALIST

THE REVIVALIST

A NOVELLA BY
PERRY SLAUGHTER

SINISTER REGARD
New York
2015

ISBN 978-1-941-92835-6

Trade paperback edition: August 2015

www.sinisterregard.com
www.perryslaughter.com

For the children,
who shall inherit the mess

THE
REVIVALIST

1

McFARLAND EDGED STIFFLY AROUND THE CROWD OF TOWNSPEO-ple massed in the giant revival tent, wiping sweat from the back of his neck. It was infernally hot. The church goons really had the space heaters cranked up, and the press of bodies was making things even worse. McFarland had noticed the welcomers opening and closing the tent flaps at regularly timed intervals, to let in a few seconds' worth of cool evening breezes. He ran his wrinkled fingers along the red-and-white-striped fiberglass fabric of the tent wall. They came away wet. Condensation.

He raised his eyebrows. That just might hold the plague tide at bay long enough to spray it down and wash it away before it could do any damage, on the off-chance that any of it blew across the moat during the revival. These churchies certainly weren't stupid.

"And I ask again, people of Wellington, Nevada," shouted the preacher, a small bearded figure dressed all in black, waving his arms as he walked up and down the raised platform at the front of the tent, "have ye been spiritually born of God? Have ye been spiritually reborn?"

A dozen voices shouted, "Yes!" A few more, "No!" Scattered others, "Amen!"

McFarland sighed. It was the evening of Good Friday; there must have been close to a thousand people crowded into the tent, not counting the preacher himself and his dozens of glaze-eyed roadies, and it was clear they had no idea how to respond. Most of them were too young to have ever seen a televangelist, let alone a traveling revival.

The preacher crouched down at the edge of the platform and pointed into the crowd. "I say unto you, nay!" he bellowed. "Have ye been filled with the fire of the Holy Spirit? Have ye received the gift of tongues? Have ye healed your fellow man, or cast out the devils from his breast? Have ye been ministered to by angels, and have the dead risen and walked at the touch of your hand?" He darted to and fro like a whippet, pointing his finger at someone new with each question. "Then I say unto you, ye have not been reborn, and ye have not tasted of the sweetness and mercy of Christ's love!"

McFarland's eyes weren't what they once had been, but he could see how the preacher's high, pale forehead dripped with sweat and reflected the light of the sodium arc lamps mounted on poles all around the platform. McFarland had tried to tune out the preaching, but it was just too loud to ignore. He peered up into the dimness where the tent's support bars criss-crossed, trying to spot the loudspeakers that had to be there. Damn, he'd give his eyeteeth for solar cells and storage batteries like these churchies must have.

And he'd give his withered left nut for five minutes with their microwave transmitter.

"For verily," the preacher went on, "Christ Jesus himself did all these things and more, and he has given unto his true followers to do the same! He healed the lame, the blind, the deaf, changed water to wine, fed thousands with a few loaves of bread!

He cast out devils, yea, even an entire host of devils who called themselves Legion! He fasted forty days, faced the sorest temptations of the Devil himself, raised the dead, and overcame even his own death when after three days in the tomb—"

"Hell of a preacher, ain't he, Carl?" said a familiar voice. "He's even got *you* starin' with your mouth open like a goddamn carp."

"Huh?" said McFarland, turning.

It was Reed Jacobson, a wizened old mechanic in his late eighties, even more ancient than McFarland himself. Jacobson had separated himself from the crowd, and he jerked a thumb in the direction of the platform. "Course, he ain't nowheres as good as your daddy used to be. Now *there* 'uz a man could put the smell o' brimstone in your nostrils the way he pounded that pulpit. But that's forty years ago."

McFarland nodded. Personally, he suspected that if there really was a hell, it would stink more like the hot sweat there inside the revival tent than it would any sulfide, but that wasn't worth getting into with old Reed. "Maybe I did get a little caught up, there," he said, "but not because I actually *believe* this rot. Preachers like this one use their words and their gestures to induce a kind of mass hypnosis."

Jacobson took off his tattered John Deere cap and scratched the liver spots on his pink scalp. "Ayuh, whatever you say. I ain't no fancy scientist. But anyways, I 'uz just gonna say you 'uz the last one I 'spected to see here to the revival."

"You think I'd miss this?" said McFarland. "Hell, Reed, these are the first other human beings we've seen in forty years. Their wagons actually made it through the plague tide without so much as a *scratch* that I can see, and I'm going to find out how they did it."

"Power o' God, if you ask me," said Jacobson with a wry, gap-toothed grin.

McFarland snorted. "They've got a microwave transmitter on one of those wagons of theirs, and they obviously know not only the right frequency but also the right signal to deactivate those damned little machines."

"You're still on one 'bout them nanny-machines o' yours?"

"*Nano*machines," said McFarland tersely. "And if you didn't believe me before, you sure as hell ought to believe me now, the way they rode into town this morning. The plague tide parted for them like they were the Israelites and it was the Red Sea."

"'Tain't a question o' believin' you or not believin' you," said Jacobson. "I mean, machines so small you cain't but see 'em less'n there's a gazillion of 'em all together? Granted, I s'pose it's possible, but it don't do me no good to *know* it, at least not 's I can see. Don't change the fact that we're here and they're all around us and we cain't go two feet past the moat without we get turned into guns or ammo or a lump o' goddamn bean curd, does it? Know what I'm sayin', Carl?"

"If you understand it, you can *fight* it."

"You been fightin' for forty years, an' it ain't got you nothin' but old an' bitter," said Jacobson. "*I'm* old an' bitter, too, but it didn't cost me near 's much. Listen, Carl"—and he squeezed McFarland's shoulder with a gnarled old hand—"God knows you're a smart fellah, but let's give this preacher here a chance. Mebbe he's got somethin' we can use."

McFarland bit off a vicious retort about the mentality of people who buy snake oil. He had a pretty good idea that any miracle the preacher and his goons had to offer would come cloaked in fantasy and ritual. Even if it kept the plague inactive, it wouldn't give the town any freedom; it would only enslave them to superstition. That was the reason McFarland had bothered to show up at all, either to debunk the preacher and his so-called new religion, or to steal whatever secrets were locked up in those wagons for the common good of the town—both, if possible.

"Does God love his children here cut off from the world in Wellington, Nevada?" roared the preacher. A few voices cried out in the affirmative. "Yes, of course he does! How does he show it? By *correcting* them when they've gone astray! And are the people of Wellington, Nevada, being corrected by their God? I say unto you, *yea*—yea, whom the Lord loveth, he chastiseth, and whom the Lord loveth, he testeth! My dear sisters and brothers"—and here the preacher's voice dropped as he sadly shook his head—"never have I seen so sore a correction, so sore a test, as that which has afflicted Wellington, Nevada, and indeed this entire great land, for the past *forty years!*"

A score of hallelujahs, mostly from the oldtimers, rose into the air. Jacobson waved his soiled cap, shouting, and McFarland's lip curled in disgust. Anyone old enough to walk before the plague hit should know better than this.

"For my friends, we as a community, as a nation, perhaps as a world, are under as severe a condemnation as ever God has seen fit to visit upon his children in his wrath and in his mercy! Our homes, our crops, our cities and towns, our forests and our deserts and our wildlife—even our very loved ones, should they venture beyond the safety of the community—are transformed before our eyes, even as Lot's wife of old, into manna on the one hand, the very staff of life, or on the other into diabolical weapons of war!"

A hush descended as the preacher turned his eyes upward. "My friends, God in his infinite wisdom has handed us in equal measure the means of our salvation and the means to our destruction. Never in the history of man has the choice been so clear. Partake of the staff of life, and live. Partake of the weapons of destruction—*and die the eternal death, which is everlasting damnation!*" The preacher's face turned a deep red in his righteous anger, and even from the back of the crowd McFarland could see the veins bulging in his forehead.

Then the shaking of his upraised fist subsided, and his voice softened once again. "Brothers, sisters, the fact that you are here tonight to partake of the sweet nectar of his Spirit attests to the fact that you have chosen the better path, fought the better fight. And in his compassion, Jesus Christ, our holy Lord and Master, has sent me, his chosen prophet, here to you, in humble Wellington, Nevada, to partake of his rebirth, and to show you the way to life everlasting."

McFarland had had all he could take, and he marched toward the tent's wide center aisle wearing a scowl of fierce indignation. Jacobson, his face bloodless, grabbed at McFarland's bony wrist as he passed. "Carl, for Pete's sake, whaddaya think you're—"

McFarland shook his arm free. "Shut up, Reed, you damned old fool," he hissed, and then he was standing at the head of the center aisle, where a dozen stout churchies of both sexes in a wide double line held the crowd in place like the posts of a fence. "What's the catch?" he shouted, planting his fists on his hips. "What are we going to owe you for this great benevolent service?"

His voice squeaked at the end, but no one was laughing. The crowd was murmuring as their eyes turned toward him, and he felt only hostility from all these hundreds of people he had worked so hard to save from ignorance and death. But he stood his ground, not meeting anyone's eyes, just staring coldly at the preacher on his platform. He felt like a parent to these people, and no one was going to take advantage of their lack of education, not while he was still breathing.

"Well, friend, you will owe *me* nothing," said the preacher with an easy smile, spreading his arms and bowing slightly. His beard was very black, trimmed thin along the jawline. "But you will owe *God* your love, your worship, and your obedience."

"And who dictates the form that obedience takes?" McFarland said loudly. "You?"

The eyes of the crowd swept to McFarland and back to the preacher again, who snatched up a leather-bound Bible from a stool standing close by. "*This!* The word of all the holy prophets throughout all the ages of man!"

"I thought *you* were a prophet! Why rely on the Bible if God talks to you one on one?"

A babble arose, and McFarland heard more than one cry of "Shut up and sit down!" But the preacher motioned for the crowd to be still. "My brothers and sisters, my children, hold. Why not let our elder friend talk? How better to teach a man his errors than to catch him in his words? How better to silence the Devil than to catch him out in his lies? Come forward, oldtimer. You have nothing to fear from us, nor we from you, so let's converse like civilized friends." He gestured encouragingly. "Come on."

A queer, cold fear filled McFarland's belly, but no way he was going to back down now. As he walked up the center aisle, the preacher's goons tracked him with their glazed eyes, but none of them moved. The townspeople, however, couldn't keep themselves silent, and there were hisses and a few catcalls. "Don't you screw this up for us, McFarland," said a voice from out of the babble, and McFarland turned his head to see Jed Thomas, head of the town council, watching him angrily from an aisle seat. McFarland, hands at his sides, gave Thomas the finger as he passed by.

Then he was at the platform, under the blinding sodium arc lamps, squinting as two burly churchies helped him climb up.

As McFarland got to his feet on the scuffed pine planking, eyes watering, he felt very old and frail and vulnerable. The preacher shook him by the hand, and though the man's smile was wide, his eyes were cold and hard and blue as ice. McFarland was very conscious of the contrast between his patched overalls and grungy woolen shirt, and the preacher's pressed black suit, black blouse, and white collar.

"So, oldtimer," the preacher said, his voice booming from all sides of the tent, "tell me—exactly how old *are* you?"

McFarland bristled, but he said evenly, "Eighty, this February just past." He wanted to cross his arms in front of his chest to ward off the feeling of nakedness brought on by the harsh lights and the vast crowd, but he resisted. He wasn't going to be the one squirming; he aimed to make this so-called holy man squirm.

"So you had grown to your manhood in the times before the plague?"

The delayed echo of the preacher's voice made McFarland's head hurt. Squinting, he could make out fibers of gray in the man's black, slicked-back hair. He also spotted the matte-black microphone clipped to the lapel of his black suit jacket. McFarland leaned close and said, loudly, "I must have been forty to your five when the plague hit, yes."

His thin voice boomed as loudly as the preacher's had, and a handful of people in the audience laughed at the expression of surprise on the preacher's face. McFarland tried to hide a grin; he thought he might be starting to enjoy this.

The preacher smiled good-naturedly, but his eyes were still cold. "You have witnessed, then, in the maturity of your eyes and your soul, the ways in which the simplest works of God tear down and make dust of the mightiest works of the twenty-first century's mightiest nation of men."

McFarland leaned in toward the mike again. "If you're refer-ring to the plague tide in that roundabout way of yours, then the works of God don't make dust of things—they make tofu and Tommy guns." There was more laughter. "But you haven't con-vinced me it's a work of God."

The preacher smiled through clenched teeth. "Are you saying you don't . . . believe . . . in . . . God?"

"I believe there's a basic order and harmony underlying the universe," said McFarland, "maybe even a First Cause, a Prime Mover. I don't know if that's God or not. But I know that if there *is* a God, then my father, the finest man ever to preach from any pulpit in this town, was a *man* of that God, and he nev-er for one moment would have countenanced the kind of tech-nological smokescreen you're trying to foist off on this town as a miracle, as a—as an evidence of your power."

Murmurs of agreement drifted up from the crowd, mixed equally with shouts of ridicule.

"So, if I am to understand you correctly," said the preacher with force, silencing the audience, "this plague that afflicts us is *not* a punishment, *not* a loving correction from our Lord—and *I* have not been granted the power to part that dread tide that my followers and I may pass safely through?" He stroked his beard, then turned and paced across the platform. At the far edge he turned again and regarded McFarland blandly. "How then do you explain the fact that we—and we alone in forty years—have arrived here safely in your little town?"

McFarland was acutely aware that he had lost the advantage of the preacher's microphone, so he raised his voice and hoped it wouldn't squeak. "I never said you don't have the power to pass safely through the plague. I'm just not convinced it was God who gave you that power."

"Who then?" said the preacher with raised eyebrows. "Surely not the Devil?"

"No, not him, either," said McFarland, "even though I see plenty of evidence for *his* existence here tonight."

The preacher ignored the slur. "Again, then who?"

McFarland pursed his lips. How much of his hand should he play? He decided to err on the side of recklessness, match the preacher's brashness with a brashness of his own. "The United States Army," said McFarland distinctly.

The crowd was silent, and for a moment the preacher seemed to stunned to speak. But he recovered quickly, letting go an amused laugh that seemed genuine. "My dear friend," he said, "I have carried my message from one end of this continent to the other and back again, and there is no longer even a United States to speak of, let alone an army to defend it. What ever could lead you to such a patently ridiculous conclusion?"

The townspeople were murmuring again, and McFarland had to speak his very loudest to make them hear. "Because I worked for them before the plague." Sweat plastered his shirt to his back, and a dizziness born of the heat and the lights washed up him in a prickly wave. But the crowd quieted down somewhat, and with a deep breath McFarland plunged ahead: "I actually worked for a research consortium based out of MIT, but essentially all we did was contractual work for the military. Our specialty was nano-technology."

The preacher managed to look both puzzled and amused at the same time. "Please enlighten us poor, ignorant souls, my friend. What is this 'nanotechnology' you speak of so glibly?"

McFarland had to raise his voice again. "I think most every-one here has put up with me trying to explain it to them before, and I'm sure you know all about it yourself, but I'll go ahead and play along. Nanotechnology is the science of building tiny machines, molecule by molecule, which are capable of manipulating matter on its most fundamental levels."

"Tiny machines," repeated the preacher. "Tiny machines." He clasped his hands again behind his back and stood at the edge of the platform with his head bowed, as if in deep thought. "And how tiny do you mean when you say that? As tiny as, say, a mouse? As tiny as my thumbnail? Tiny as a grain of sand, perhaps?" He asked this last question with a wry smile.

"No, sir. As I'm sure you realize, I'm talking about machines so tiny you couldn't see a million of them—a *billion* of them—even if they were all lumped together in a ball. Some as small as complex molecules."

"Ah, I see." The preacher gave the crowd a broad wink, and they laughed appreciatively. "Well, now that we're clear on *that*, please continue with this fascinating *little* fantasy."

McFarland's hands clenched into fists, but he kept his voice under control. "I was involved in a separate undertaking, but I saw the preliminary specs for something called 'Project Scorched Earth.'" He suddenly had difficulty speaking, and his vision began to blur. He blinked furiously, mouth tight. "The design encompassed a linked system of mobile nanocomputers, assemblers, disassemblers, and replicators, which would be released into a clearly delineated battlefield area. There they would gather raw materials, build copies of themselves, and set about dismantling the entire landscape. Trees, houses, factories—even animals and people. Everything taken apart at the molecular level. The constituent molecules—especially the carbon, hydrogen, oxygen, and nitrogen—would then be used to assemble food and weapons for the occupying forces."

"*Assemble* food?" said the preacher with a harsh bark of laughter. "My friend, one does not *assemble* food as if it were a house or a wagon! Why, what role is God left to play in your—"

"God does it the *exact* same way!" shouted McFarland, beginning to feel light-headed. "The cells in plants and animals—hell, in our own bodies—are nothing more than naturally occurring molecular machines! They take carbon and oxygen and all the rest of it and put it together into living tissue! We learned how to do it, too! My God, the evidence is right out there for anyone to see!"

"Then you claim to have usurped the role of God *himself?*" demanded the preacher in sudden anger.

"Maybe that's what we did!" cried McFarland, feeling a buried, snarling anguish rise up inside him. "Maybe *that's* what we're being punished for! But if I had the means to stop this plague, I sure as *hell* wouldn't hide it behind a bunch of pseudoreligious mumbo-jumbo and call myself a prophet!"

The crowd was on its feet now, shouting. The stone-faced churchies fought to hold people back in the front rows, and McFarland knew he'd pushed his luck a little too far. He was going to be lynched. But he had his momentum; he couldn't stop himself now. He strode right up to the preacher where the mike would pick up his voice and shouted, "There's a radio signal that'll stop those things cold, and dammit, you know what it is! Why don't you just *give* it to us—"

"*Silence!*" roared the preacher, and the word reverberated from every corner of the tent, like a pronouncement from God.

The crowd fell still. McFarland shrank back as if he'd been whipped. The preacher was red, trembling with rage, and the vein in his forehead throbbed like a pulsing tongue of flame. "You claim I have some kind of demonic mastery over a plague decreed by the mouth of Christ the Lord?"

The lights, the heat, the noise all battered at McFarland like a physical assault. He could barely hear his own voice when he said, "I do."

"I am the mouthpiece of God!" cried the preacher with the fury of a destroying angel, pointing a stiff arm and burning gaze at McFarland. "I am his right arm! I am the instrument of his judgment on this earth, his flaming sword of righteousness! I have no need of trickery while the fire of his Holy Spirit fills me like a cleansing wind!"

And McFarland found a small island of clarity in the center of all that concentrated rage. "Prove it," he said levelly, tottering on the edge of collapse. "Show me a miracle."

The preacher's eyes smoldered. "Will ye tempt even God then?" he said, his voice a terrifying hiss. "Wilt thou ask for a sign when thou hast had signs enough?" But then his demeanor changed subtly, and he nodded as if struck by a cruel inspiration. "I am grieved by the hardness of your heart. But even so, thou shalt have thy miracle, for it is better that thy soul should be lost than that thou shouldst be the means of bringing many souls down to destruction by thy lying and flattering words. Thou shalt see the powers of life and death which God hath committed into my hands. Thou shalt witness the miraculous rebirth which God hath promised unto all those who come unto him with broken hearts and contrite spirits!"

Then he raised both arms high above his head and cried, "Bring unto me your dead!"

The largest flap at the back of the tent opened, and four of the preacher's church goons entered, bearing on their shoulders the body of a thirtyish woman. They carried their burden up the center aisle without haste. Dread and excitement rippled through the crowd, and McFarland heard one high, distraught voice clearly above the rest: "Martha! God's mama, *Martha!*"

The bearers were close enough now that McFarland could recognize the body. It was Martha Stillman, who had passed away the day before during a breach delivery. McFarland could make out Bob Stillman in the audience, still shouting incoherently. He had pressed his infant son into the arms of someone nearby and was fighting his way toward the aisle.

On Sunday morning, after the three days set aside for grieving had passed, Martha's body was to be placed on the far side of the moat—with any luck, to be turned into food for the benefit of the community.

The bearers laid the body gently down on the platform between McFarland and the preacher, so its feet were pointing toward the crowd, then headed back down the aisle. Two of them stopped to restrain Bob Stillman, who continued to call out his wife's name, tears streaking his cheeks.

Martha's body was clothed in a denim dress that had been mended so many times that there were more patches than original fabric. Her white, curled feet were bare. She had been a handsome woman in life, but tired, and it tore McFarland's heart to realize that she didn't look much different dead than she had alive.

He thought of his wife Eileen and their beautiful daughter Hillary, both of whom he had lost in the first winter of the plague . . .

He felt faint.

The preacher raised his arms again and bowed his head, and to McFarland's tear-blurred vision there were two preachers, then four. "Our most merciful Lord and Savior Jesus Christ," intoned the preacher. "I call upon thee in thy unmatched glory and wisdom to grant unto me, thy humble and simple servant, power even unto the confounding of the wisdom of men, that

I may bring down the spirit of doubt and unbelief which doth hang over this gathering, and show forth thy mercy and love, which will lead us all unto salvation and rebirth in thy holiest of kingdoms. Amen."

A chorus of amens drifted up from the audience, and the preacher dropped to his knees beside Martha Stillman's body. McFarland caught what might have been the gleam of something plastic in the palm of the preacher's hand, but then the man was cupping his hands gently to the sides of Martha's neck, and he cried out, "Awake, thou who sleepest, and arise!" and stood up again with a flourish of his hands.

And the body on the platform trembled, and its eyes fluttered open, and the preacher put out his hand and helped Martha Stillman stand as she blinked around herself in confusion, and with a shout Bob Stillman broke free of the churchies holding him back, and suddenly the heat and the lights and the din of the hallelujahs were all too much for McFarland and he slumped to the planks in a heap.

2

"So in other words," said McFarland, scribbling madly with his finger on the chalkboard-sized LCD slate, "to deliver the same amount of physical power, a piece of 240-volt equipment can be supplied by a wire with only half the diameter of the one supplying a piece of 120-volt equipment." The slate was one of the few pre-plague artifacts sanctioned by the town council for private use, but that was due only to its low power rating, not to any benefit they could see in the classes McFarland taught.

He surveyed the simple equations, then turned from the slate to face the two students slumped in the sprung couch that was the only major piece of furniture in his living room besides a pair of sagging bookcases. "Any questions?" he said, but the abstracted expression in Rachel's eyes told him that the morning's lecture was going nowhere. Orrin seemed attentive—but then, Orrin *always* seemed attentive, even when he was bored stiff.

McFarland sighed, then peeled off the wire-rimmed glasses he used for reading and other close work. They came from the community pool at the town hall, and the frames had been soldered in a few places. He'd have to see about trading them in for stronger pair soon; his close vision was deteriorating fast.

"Okay, okay," he said, clearing the slate with a wave of his hand. "I know no one's interested in electricity on a Saturday morning. We shouldn't even have tried to hold class with only two of you here." He drummed his fingers on his stomach. "But you bothered to come. Now, what do you *really* want to talk about?"

Rachel Ivie checked her watch, an old mechanical thing that her father must have secured for her as soon as it entered the community pool. "Well," she said, "I can't stay a whole lot longer anyway because I promised my mother I'd go to that youth Bible workshop at the revival tent this morning." She smoothed her long red hair back over one ear with a gesture that was graceful and endearing. She had recently turned sixteen and was just beginning to be comfortable with her new woman's body. McFarland was of an age where he could appreciate her beauty without feeling any untoward yearnings. "But *I* want to know about this radio signal thing you were talking about last night."

"We've been keeping that kind of a secret, because we didn't want to get anyone's hopes up," said McFarland, glancing slyly at Orrin, "but I suppose I did let the cat out of the bag. Orrin, do you want to do the honors?"

"S-sure." Orrin Pritchard shifted clumsily on the couch, finding it seemingly impossible to arrange his long limbs in a comfortable position. He was a gangly, dark-haired nineteen-year-old, and McFarland found the young man's crush on Rachel almost painful to observe in its poignancy and hopelessness. Behind his stammer, though, was keen mind, and Orrin was the closest thing to a friend McFarland had had in this town for years. "W-w-we all know that the p-plague is attracted to any source of r-radio waves. According to C-C-Carl, the Army designed it that way so it would kn-kn-knock out enemy communications before a-anything else."

Orrin looked to McFarland as if for encouragement, and McFarland nodded. Orrin continued: "But there was a c-c-certain frequency set aside that *wouldn't* have that effect—n-not actually a radio signal, but d-d-down in the microwave range, with a w-wavelength of about a m-millimeter and a half. We i-i-isolated it through tr-trial and error. S-s-signals at *that* f-f-frequency have the same general effect on the plague t-tide as liquid w-w-water, except the plague stays inactive only for the d-duration of the s-signal, not for t-t-twenty-four hours like with water."

"So why haven't you told everyone about this?" said Rachel. Her green eyes danced with excitement, but her arms were folded sternly beneath her breasts. "I mean, we can control the plague now, right? All you need is a bunch of transmitters set up around town!"

"W-w-w-w-well, th-th-th-th—" stammered Orrin. He blew out his breath, flustered and red-faced.

McFarland took over smoothly, and Orrin breathed a sigh. "That's the difficulty. Radio transmitters aren't so hard to build, but we need *microwave* transmitters. Now, I've managed to build *one*, from pieces of an old microwave oven, but I don't think we'll be able to scavenge many more like it, and at any rate it's not near powerful enough for what we need. Orrin and I have done a few experiments with it across the moat, but its signal radius is really pretty pathetic."

Rachel raised an eyebrow at Orrin, seeming impressed, and Orrin squared his shoulders a little.

"Anyway," said McFarland, "knowing the right frequency is only half the battle. According to the specs I saw for Project Scorched Earth, there was a special signal, some kind of digital code, that would totally deactivate the nanomachines. Forever. They'd flood the battlefield with this signal before sending troops in, once the plague had done its work. Unfortunately, the code was at least a million bits long, probably orders of magnitude more, and it was non-repeating. If we could reproduce that code, then even with one little transmitter we'd be able to at least make some inroads into the plague tide, travel around, explore a little. But there's no hope of that. Even if we had the right equipment, it would take longer than the life of the universe to try every combination of bits."

"But this p-p-preacher," said Orrin. "H-h-*he* has the code! He m-must!"

McFarland nodded. "All the right equipment, too. How else could he and his goons have reached us here?"

"Hey," said Rachel, "they're not goons—at least not all of them. I talked to one for a while last night, and he was really nice."

McFarland's mouth narrowed. He noted the hurt in Orrin's eyes. "This . . . churchie," said McFarland. "He's not going to be at the Bible workshop, is he?"

Now it was Rachel who flushed. She looked down at her lap, a traitorous smile playing at the corners of her mouth. "Of course he is. They're *all* going to be there."

"I *thought* you a were a little eager to obey your mother," McFarland said, half to himself. "Listen to me for a second, Rachel. Listen to me!"

Her head snapped up at the quiet force in his voice. She looked as if she had been slapped. McFarland rarely used that tone of voice with his students, but he wanted to make an impression on her. "These could turn out to be very dangerous people," he said. "I don't know exactly what their angle is yet, but I'd make sure not to end up alone with any of them, especially the ones with that glazed sort of look in their eyes."

"That's an *otherworldly* look," said Rachel hotly, cheeks blazing. "Jeff sees realms, higher planes, that the rest of us aren't *aware* enough to perceive!"

"So you're already on a first-name basis with this nice young Christian of yours." McFarland tried to keep the sarcasm out of his voice, but failed.

Rachel stood up. "He and his people are here to *help* us—which is more than I can say for anyone in this room." She marched stiffly to the front door. "See you both at the revival tonight."

With a few quick steps, McFarland managed to catch the door before it slammed. Orrin struggled up from the couch and followed McFarland out onto the porch. "Rachel!" called McFarland, but there was no reply. Together they watched her receding back disappear below the curve of the hill.

McFarland sagged against one of the posts that supported the eaves of the house. A stiff breeze tousled his sparse, white hair. "Damn," he said. "Sending her off in a righteous huff was the *last* thing I wanted to do."

"It wasn't your f-f-fault," said Orrin, behind him. There was real pain in his voice.

"Come sit down with me, Orrin. There must be a storm blowing in, because my joints are starting to ache something fierce. My knees, especially." McFarland descended the steps to the walk, then crossed the grass toward a large, flat boulder that was his favorite place to sit. "Did you notice anything odd about Rachel's choice of topics back there?"

"Y-you mean when your l-l-lesson pretty much ground to a halt?"

"That's right," McFarland said gruffly, lowering himself onto the boulder. Orrin took a seat beside him.

Orrin, pondering, sat down beside him, and as the young man considered the question McFarland regarded the view. Wellington sat nestled in the eastern foothills of the Sierra Nevada, about ten miles from the California state line and perhaps forty miles southeast of Lake Tahoe. The west fork of the Walker River tumbled past Wellington on its way to Walker Lake in the far-distant valley, and in the desert to the east of the lake lay the richest silver-mining lands in the country. Of course, *everything* outside the moat was desert now—littered with the creations of the plague—but McFarland could remember how it had been in the eighties and nineties when he was growing up, forests of pine and spruce blanketing the hillsides, mule deer nibbling leaves from the willows and aspen in the front yard, raccoons pawing through the garbage cans at night. He recalled those years now in a romantic light, though he had hated Wellington as a boy.

The house where he had grown up, now his own house, sat isolated on a ridge overlooking the rest of town. Only his nearly forgotten status as Wellington's savior permitted him to keep it; most of the town's seventeen hundred residents were crammed into the city center, two and three families to a house, to conserve light and heat and to make for a swifter response in the event of an emergency. Far off to McFarland's left raced the Walker, swollen with melted snow, and to his right ran the man-made canal that branched off from the river high above, curved in a broad sweep around the town and its acres of farmlands, and rejoined the river below. Inside this circle, all was green and lush, thick with grass and trees and the beginnings of the spring planting. Outside, there was only a shimmering, silver-gray wasteland that gave way in places to tracts of bare, grayish rock.

Heavy clouds were pushing their way from the west over the mountains at his back, while to the east the entire sky was veiled by a thin layer of cirrostratus that weakened the midmorning sun. McFarland could pick out a few dozen figures in the wastes east of town, spraying water from tanks strapped to their backs to forge a safe trail through the plague tide as they hunted for manna. Most of the oldtimers still called it tofu, though it was higher in nutrition and even more devoid of taste than natural bean curd, but the Biblical name had caught on among the younger generation and would only be reinforced by this mad series of revivals.

In a fallow field to the southeast, near the pens where the goats and sheep were bred, bloomed the revival tent, its red stripes like rivulets of blood soaking the soil. Nearby was the ring of old circus wagons which had brought the preacher and his goons across the desert, and from this vantage McFarland could see the deep-black radiance of the solar panels that lay atop them. A score of horses were tethered nearby. Dozens of people milled about in the field, townsfolk and churchies alike, and it looked as if there might be some kind of cookout going on.

Farther on, across the moat in the wasteland, sat one lone wagon in the middle of an island of gray rock. The silvery shimmer of the plague curved well away from this wagon.

That was where the microwave equipment would be.

"Well?" said McFarland to the young man beside him.

The wind from down the hillside, thick with the scent of rain, lifted Orrin's hair. "It's s-s-strange to me that Rachel only w-wanted to hear about the radio signal," he said. "I'd have th-th-thought she'd be bursting with qu-questions about Martha Stillman. I know *I* am."

McFarland stared bleakly at the goings-on at the tent far below. "As am I. It really worries me, in fact." He ran a gnarled hand through his hair. "I mean, it's as if she, and probably most of the other young people in this town, has such a skewed sense of reality that the sight of a woman rising up from the dead doesn't raise a single question in her mind, a kernel of skepticism. She just accepts it." He sighed. "Not that I can really blame her. Hell, her *parents* don't even remember what things were like before the plague. It's no surprise a miracle doesn't faze her. She has no point of reference to tell her the way things really work."

"I g-grew up the same way," said Orrin.

"Well, your father's pushing sixty. *He* remembers. I think a healthy skepticism must have rubbed off on you. But the rest of this town . . ." He shook his head ruefully. "I mean, no one here gives a *damn* about science. I offer classes so there'll be people who know how things operate after I'm gone, and I get maybe eight students on a good day—and hell, most of those are only here to get out of food-gathering. No one *cares*. No one realizes how *precarious* our position here is." He exhaled sharply. "This traveling charlatan's going to fleece this town like a flock of sheep. If he makes us careless, makes us relax our vigilance for *one* hour . . ." McFarland let the thought hang, too worked up to go on.

Orrin started to say something, stopped, then started again: "D-d-do you know how he did it? Resurrected M-Mrs. Stillman, I mean?"

McFarland laughed. "I was wondering how long it'd take you to work up the nerve to ask that." But then he grew serious again. "I have an idea, yes, a pretty good one . . . but before I know for certain I'll have to make a little social call on the Stillman family. See how they've been lately." He levered himself to his feet. "Like to come along?"

Orrin squinted at the sun, a look of disappointment on his face. "I-I-I'm on the honeypot p-patrol this morning. I have to be g-g-getting down there soon."

McFarland made a face. "Tough break." The town couldn't afford to waste water on flushing away sewage, so all waste products were collected and then dumped outside the moat to be broken down by the plague tide and reassembled into food. "Why don't you walk with me as far as downtown, at least?"

As Orrin stood, McFarland felt a sudden urge to invite him back up to the house for a glass of goats' milk and a few hands of gin rummy. They didn't get a chance to play much lately, and he was sure Orrin could use a short escape as much as he could. But McFarland understood his own tendency to want to put off things that needed to be done, especially difficult things. If he and Orrin started playing cards and drinking milk, it could be hours before they decided to quit. It had happened more than once.

McFarland grunted and started off toward the path.

The freshening wind at their backs helped speed them along, and before they had hiked down below the ridge McFarland glanced over his shoulder to see how the wind turbines were running. The wind from the small canyon above Wellington was nearly constant year-round, and early on McFarland had supervised the construction of the tall turbines. There were several dozen, marching strategically down from the mouth of the canyon, built from lumber and parts scavenged from the local electrical substation. Together with a water turbine on the river near town and few solar panels from before the plague, these provided all Wellington's electricity.

McFarland leaned on Orrin's arm as they descended the steepest part of the path. "By the way," he said, "thanks for helping me home last night. At least, I assume it was you. I don't remember anything from the time I blacked out until I woke up in my own bed this morning."

"It was m-me and Reed Jacobson and a c-couple of others," said Orrin. "You were r-r-really out of it. I was afraid you'd bumped your h-head and gone into a coma."

"When I woke up, I thought I'd dreamed the whole thing—the revival, the preacher, everything. I remember some kind of argument . . ."

Orrin looked grim. "The ch-ch-church people wanted to take you back to one of their w-wagons when you passed out. They said they could t-t-take better care of you there than anyone in town c-could. I wouldn't let them." He looked away, abashed. "I was the f-first one to reach you."

"Thank you, Orrin," said McFarland softly, feeling a tightness in his throat. "I don't think those churchies meant me any goodwill. I doubt they're too fond of me after the fuss I raised up there on stage."

They were passing through a stand of cottonwoods, the foundations of cannibalized houses visible on either side of the path, and McFarland was silent for a few moments. The light was gray and the air very still. He stopped walking. "Orrin, depending on what I find out at the Stillmans' place, I may have a surprise of my own to trot out at tonight's revival. Are you going to be there?"

Orrin shook his head. "I'm afraid t-today's my big day for community service. I'm on the p-p-perimeter this afternoon and this evening."

"Actually, that's probably just as well." McFarland rubbed his chin. "Listen, are you in this with me? Do you want to see this preacher discredited as much as I do? Do you want access to all the technology he's got locked away in those wagons of his?"

"I-I-I *think* so," said Orrin, not quite meeting McFarland's eyes. But after a moment of hard thought his gaze solidified. "No . . . no, *yes*. Yes, I do."

"Good." McFarland was satisfied as to Orrin's sincerity. The boy had iron in him; it just took him a while to find it. "Now, as far as we know, these churchies are in town for two more nights. At least, that's what they've led us to believe. Who knows if they're planning to leave some kind of overseer or—or God-squadron behind when they go? Whatever they're planning to do, we don't have much time to head it off. Now, do you think you can get yourself stationed on the part of moat that runs between the tent and that one wagon that's still on the other side?"

"Y-yes," said Orrin. McFarland could see that he was beginning to be nervous, but trying not to show it.

"Do it, then. And I want you to keep your eyes on that wagon, especially after it gets dark. I don't think you'll have to worry about any plague getting across tonight, not with the microwaves they're pumping out. You'll be free to concentrate on the wagon itself. Don't go pointing your floodlight out there or doing anything else to draw attention to yourself, but I want to know how many people are out there, when they come and go, if there are any guards on duty, what their rounds are, when they break for a piss and when they trade shifts. If someone out there *spits* funny I want to know about it. Is that clear?"

McFarland had unconsciously slipped into the speech patterns he had heard so often when he worked with the military, and the effect on Orrin was profound. He stood up straight, choked down any misgivings he might have had, and said, "Yes, s-s-sir. I-i-is that everything?"

"For tonight," said McFarland. "We'll see how things go at the revival this evening before we make any more plans."

At the edge of town, a hundred yards further on, they parted ways.

3

June Burlingame answered the door at McFarland's knock. "Oh, it's you," she said with evident disapproval. June was a prim, tight-lipped young woman who managed to make even her gray woolen shift look as proper as a high-necked, floor-length evening gown. "To what do we owe *this* honor?" Her voice was nasal and grating.

McFarland smiled, masking his dislike of the woman. "Lovely to see you, too, Mrs. Burlingame. Is Bob or Martha in this morning?"

"Well, they *should* be at the Bible study, as should all right-minded people"—she said this with pointed stress—"but I'll go ahead and check for you." With what was certainly meant as a look of martyrdom, June retreated into the house, but not before latching the torn screen door from the inside. McFarland had noted the dark circles under her eyes.

"Thank you," he called through the screen. "Mighty Christian of you."

He shivered as he waited on the stoop. He wished he'd thought to put a jacket on before leaving the house with Orrin. The clouds were thickening to the west, dark and heavy and poised to rush down the mountainside, and the wind was picking up. A puff of dust kicked up farther down the street, and treelimbs bent in front of the small frame houses. With luck the rain would hit before the wind became strong enough to blow bits of plague down from the hills into town . . .

A few moments later June reappeared, pulling a tattered sweater around her shoulders. She clutched an old red-covered Gideons' Bible in her hand. "You'll find them and their brat downstairs," she said, unlatching the door and edging past him to descend the stoop. "Through the kitchen and to your right. Now, if you'll excuse me, I must join Mr. Burlingame at the Bible study. We'll be praying for you, Mr. McFarland. Maybe the sight of that woman back from the dead will knock some light into you."

When her back was turned, McFarland bit his thumb in her general direction, then, smiling wickedly to himself, entered the house that the Burlingames shared with the Stillmans. Their living room even more sparsely furnished than his own, but it was kept neat and clean. The drapes were thrown wide open, for the townspeople had long since run out of light bulbs. A wind-up alarm clock with a cracked face sat on the mantle; electric clocks were unreliable, since the town's power was rarely delivered at a constant sixty cycles per second. As he passed through the kitchen, McFarland noticed that the sink had lost most of its enamel; rust bloomed like fading flowers on the black iron underneath. The faucet was missing.

He paused a few steps down the staircase. "Mr. Stillman?" he said.

"Yeah?" came the thick, slurred reply.

"It's Carl McFarland. I wonder if I might talk to you and your wife for a few minutes."

"Shore, c'mon down. But keep a damper on the noise. The

kid's a-sleepin' fer the firs' time in hours. Or leastwise, he's shut up fer now."

McFarland descended the dark, rickety staircase with care, not because he was worried about the noise—Stillman's voice was loud enough for someone in the attic to hear—but because his knees were really starting to smart and he was worried about tumbling to the bottom and maybe breaking a hip. He emerged into what had once been a cozy family room, with rich wood paneling on the walls and a natural-gas fireplace. Now water spots stained the acoustic tiles of the ceiling, the throw rug was full of holes, and the paneling had warped and splintered. "Siddown," said Stillman companionably, indicating a torn love seat. He was slouched in a vinyl easy chair that looked as if it had been flayed, a bottle of wine clutched in his hand.

McFarland sat gingerly in the love seat. Thin light washed into the room through a dirty casement window set high in the opposite wall. "How are you, Mr. Stillman?"

"Oh, fine, fine," said Stillman. He was in his late thirties, unshaven, and the front of his T-shirt was pale red with spilled wine. "Hey, you really socked it t' that ol' priest there last night, McFarlan'. *Some* kinda show, wudn't it?"

"Some show," said McFarland. The wine looked fairly expensive; he wondered how Stillman had gotten hold of it. Probably broke into the secret Burlingame family wine cellar. McFarland sat forward with his hands on his knees. "Mr. Stillman, how is your wife? Is she all right?"

"Martha?" Stillman took a drink from the bottle, then waved a careless hand. "Oh, yeah, she's fine, fine. Baby's fine, too, cute as a bug. Hey, care fer a nip?" He offered McFarland the bottle.

It was a tempting idea—his joints could certainly have done with it—but McFarland shook his head. "Listen, does Martha seem . . . all right to you? The way she did before?"

"Before?" Stillman seemed to grapple with the word. When he spoke again his tone was nonchalant, but his eyes seemed to betray some worry. "Oh, you wouldn't b'lieve how good she been since the baby came. Why—"

"Mr. Stillman . . . Bob . . . could I see her for a minute, do you think? I'd like to make sure she's all right, after the difficult delivery and all."

The man's eyes flickered nervously. "Shore, shore. She'd pro'bly like that. Hey, Martha," he called. "Whyn't you come on out here fer a bit?"

After a moment or two, an inner door opened and Martha Stillman moved silently into the room. She was humming to herself, and she didn't seem to be looking at anything in partic-ular. She closed the door behind her.

"Martha, Mr. McFarlan' here—"

"Hello, Mr. McFarland," she said, though she still wasn't looking at him. "I recognize you. I do. I've seen you around town many times." Her hands were clasped together in front of her, and her fingers moved in abstract little patterns. "I recognize you, too, Robert. You haven't moved from where you've been sit-ting all night."

McFarland saw now how bloodshot Stillman's darting eyes were. The man licked his lips, and the fingers of his free hand drummed on the arm of his chair. "How's li'l Bobby?" Stillman asked.

"Sleeping," said Martha. A strand of limp, wheat-colored hair had fallen across her face, and she smoothed it back with a fluid motion that had the clarity of a movie image shot at a thousand frames per second. Her skin was pale with faint blotches; the blotches seemed to pulsate.

His heart pounding, McFarland stood. He held up a hand, palm forward, and wiggled it back and forth very slightly. "Martha," he said, "can you see my hand?"

"Yes."

"Which hand am I holding up?"

"Your right hand," she said.

McFarland suppressed a shiver. Her eyes weren't even focused, let alone looking in his direction. He continued to wiggle his hand. "Is my hand moving, or is it still?"

"Still."

Goosebumps covered McFarland's arms. Stillman took a long pull at his wine bottle. "Martha," said McFarland, breathing deeply, "*Montezuma!*"

The word was a sharp bark. The look in Martha's eyes turned hard.

Stillman pulled his feet up into his chair, beginning to look genuinely frightened.

McFarland swayed on his feet. He was dizzy, feeling long, empty years peel away. "Martha!" he said, using that same sharp voice of command. "Turn in a complete circle!"

She spun, the skirts of her denim dress lifting a bit. When she had turned through exactly three hundred sixty degrees, she snapped to a halt.

"No," said Stillman softly, shaking his head. "No, no, no, no, no . . ."

"Stand on one leg!" barked McFarland.

Immediately Martha's right leg lifted. She stood like a flamingo.

"Put down your leg!"

She did.

Tears leaked from the corners of Stillman's eyes as he huddled in his easy chair, clutching the bottle as if it were a security blanket. McFarland felt a stab of guilt at robbing the man's wife of her dignity. "Bob," he said gently, "this isn't your wife. At least, not anymore."

"It is!" Stillman cried. His body shuddered with suppressed sobs. "It is!"

McFarland's own eyes started to burn. "It's not. Your wife died two days ago. This is only her body, her dead body."

"It's not, it's—"

"Bob! Listen to me!" McFarland's lips curled with revulsion, not at Stillman or his undead wife, but at himself. "Martha!" he said, forcing the words out. "Take off your dress!"

Without a flicker of emotion or hesitation, Martha began undoing the buttons down the front of her dress.

"Would your wife do that, Bob?" said McFarland, more harshly than he meant to. "Would your wife undress for me?"

"No," said Stillman, weakly, weeping, "no," but McFarland couldn't tell if he were answering the question or denying what he saw.

"Is this your wife, Bob?"

Martha's dress was undone to her navel, and the curves of a nursing bra that had been washed so many times it had turned gray were visible. She shrugged the dress from her shoulders.

"No!" cried Stillman. "I know, I know, I know!"

McFarland turned away from them both, trembling. "Martha!" he said. "Put your dress back on!"

After a few moments, he faced them again. Martha, clothed, stood as motionless as a statue. Stillman sobbed in his chair. "*Tripoli!*" McFarland barked at Martha. Her eyes softened again, lost their focus.

"I knew it wudn't her anymore," said Stillman, hands pressed against his face to hide the shame of his tears. "I *knew* it. She's differ'nt. There's somethin' . . . somethin' *missin'*."

McFarland stood silently, embarrassed. Shades of Eileen rose in his mind, shades of his father.

"They wanted me t' bring her t' the Bible class this mornin' fer ev'ryone to see, but I couldn't, I jus' couldn't. This is s'posed t' be some kinda big mir'cle? Well, lemme tell you, mister, it *ain't*. It jus' ain't."

"I know," said McFarland. "I know."

A few moments of silence passed. Stillman sniffled and wiped roughly at his face. McFarland tried to think of a graceful way to leave.

"Would you like to see my baby, Mr. McFarland?" said Martha suddenly.

Stillman turned pale. He took another drink of his wine. McFarland felt a crawling sensation at the back of his neck.

"He's sleeping now—I told you that—but you can still see him," Martha said. "He's very beautiful."

"I—I'm sure he is, Martha," said McFarland slowly. He'd confirmed his suspicions, and now there were things he needed to do. He didn't want to stay any longer.

"You don't wanna wake him, Martha," Stillman said. "You had such a hard time gettin' him t' sleep in the firs' place." He was shaking again, but this time McFarland could tell it was out of fear.

"He's completely exhausted. Nothing we do is going to wake him up." Martha's eyes didn't move, but McFarland felt her attention move to him. "I held his mouth against my breast, like mothers are supposed to do. I held him there and rocked him and rocked him, and I didn't put him down until after he stopped crying. I held him so tightly, so tightly. Mothers' breasts are a great comfort to little babies. I held him there until he didn't want to cry anymore. Do you think I did all right, Mr. McFarland?"

Ice filled McFarland's stomach. "I'm sure you did just fine, Martha." He wiped at a trickle of perspiration on the back of his neck. "May I see him?"

"Please."

She turned fluidly back to the door and opened it for McFarland, standing aside as he entered the dark room. He glanced at her as he passed, then looked away, chilled by her unfocused expression.

He stood for a moment, letting his eyes adjust. The room was not large, and he could make out the shape of the crib in the corner just a few steps away. The air smelled musty, underlaid with the faint reek of ammonia. He moved cautiously in the darkness, looked down into the crib.

The tiny infant lay on its stomach. Its back rose and fell in rhythm with its deep, even breathing.

"Such perfect little hands and feet," said Martha, peering over his shoulder.

McFarland nearly cried out. He hadn't heard her follow him into the room. He leaned heavily on the railing of the crib, trembling as the tension drained out of him.

"Can you believe that human beings really start out that small?" Martha said. She reached past him to stroke the child's head.

In the darkness McFarland couldn't make out much more than the fact that the baby seemed a little smaller than most newborns. Martha's vision was enhanced now; her eyes gathered and amplified light much better than his, and she could see in the infrared. McFarland wished he could see little Bobby that well. He didn't know whether or not to hope that the child would reach adulthood.

He felt his eyes misting over, and he cursed himself under his breath.

"Do you have a baby, Mr. McFarland?"

McFarland moved around her, away from the crib. "I did once."

"I certainly love mine," said Martha, and she came to him and took his hand. Her touch was cold, like a plucked chicken that had sat out to thaw for an hour. "Do you think I've done all right?"

"You've done beautifully," he said, and before his voice could crack and betray him he left the room pulled the door gently shut behind him.

Stillman looked up with wide eyes. "Your son *is* sleeping," said McFarland, not meeting the man's gaze. "You might want to change him soon, though. I'm not sure she'll remember to do it herself. And you'll want to make sure he gets plenty of goats' milk. I'm not sure how nutritious Martha's breast milk is."

The man began to say something, but McFarland was already on the stairs, heading up into the gray light of noon.

On the street outside, he hugged himself. The wind was blowing harder, and the sun was a white disk through the boiling clouds. A handful of people rounded the corner at the south end of the street, coming from the direction of the revival tent. McFarland headed north as fast as his aching legs would take him, not eager for another run-in with Wellington's pious. He turned west at the far corner. He needed to pick up some food at the town hall.

Then it would be time to get down to some serious business.

The cold seeped into him as he walked; his bones felt like

brittle iron. His thoughts kept straying back to the Stillmans in their dank basement, Bob pissing drunk and Martha walking dead. He hardly blamed the baby for crying all night, wrapped in a cold embrace and suckling at an icy teat. He wondered if Martha could even lactate, or if nursing her son was just an exercise in futility; that was one of the few bodily functions they hadn't paid much attention to back at MIT . . .

His hands balled into fists. He should never have gotten involved in something like Project Rapture. Nanotechnology had held so much potential, promised so many beneficial and revolutionary wonders . . . but while Japan and the European Community surged ahead in their researches, an uninformed and distrustful public had held American industry back to the point that only the armed forces had free rein to explore the new science. The young, idealistic physicist McFarland had once been hadn't spared a moment's thought for the cadavers his team raised from the dead; he had only counted himself fortunate to be part of research that was sure to turn the medical world upside down. Nanomachines that hunted down and destroyed cancer cells, eradicated harmful viruses from HIV to the common cold, knitted broken bones and torn muscles and severed nerves, reversed the aging process, repaired genetic defects in the DNA itself . . .

He had never once imagined a family like the Stillmans, pictured what his researches might turn them into.

In his mind he saw the disconcerting, unfocused gaze Martha Stillman had worn as she unbuttoned her dress—but the face from which those eyes stared was not Martha's. It belonged to Eileen, his wife.

The baby in the dark crib behind the door wasn't a baby at all, but their five-year-old daughter Hillary. Her skin was as cold as the tiled floor.

There was a time when he would have raised them both from the dead if he could have.

The stinging wind wrung tears from his eyes, and McFarland felt as though it were scouring decades of rotted ice away from his heart. The guilt was trickling back, like the first rivulets of stream water released by a spring thaw. He was responsible for all this—not just for the Stillmans, but for *all* of it, the plague, the death of the country, *everything.* Perhaps he hadn't been directly involved with Project Scorched Earth, but by his attitude, his complacency, his silence, he had certainly given it his approval—he and all the other scientists involved.

He sucked in cold wind until his lungs burned. How could they all have willed themselves into such blindness? How could they have ignored the possible consequences? Was the creation of an indestructible soldier such a noble and worthy goal?

McFarland was probably the only one who recognized that a second plague had struck Wellington—one he regarded more personally and intimately than the first—and in his misery he was sure it had risen up simply to haunt him.

The town hall was just ahead, a low fieldstone building with a glass façade that somehow managed to combine the rurally picturesque with the ultra-modern—or what had *been* ultra-modern in the days before the plague. There weren't many people on the street; those that were out seemed to be hurrying to get to shelter. McFarland pushed through the swinging glass doors, spiderwebbed from a rock thrown years before, then stopped in the foyer to wipe his streaming eyes.

"Stiff wind, eh?"

McFarland turned, vision blurred. James Ivie sat in his accustomed chair outside the door to the community pool. He leaned against the wall with the chair tipped back on two legs. "You got that right," said McFarland. "It's getting worse, too."

Ivie was about forty, with a square, handsome face that seemed creased in a perpetual smile. His brownish-blond hair was going to gray at the temples, and crow's-feet radiated from the corners of his eyes, but the freckles scattered across his nose and cheeks gave him a youthful appearance. A single homemade crutch rested beside him on the floor. His left pantleg hung emptily in front of the chair. "Looks pretty cold out there," he said, letting the chair rock back to the floor. "You after a jacket?"

McFarland shook his head. "Just a little food for the next couple of days, and some milk."

"Well, if you need anything, I'm here."

"Thanks, Jim."

McFarland pushed through another door into a reception area which, along with the offices behind it, had been converted into a storage area. A rickety wooden counter divided the room, and a pen-operated notebook computer, probably the only one in town that still ran, sat open on the countertop. McFarland rang the bell that rested beside the computer. After a few moments Silvia Gonsalves, a thick, matronly woman with dark hair swept back in a bun, appeared from the back room. Her eyes narrowed when she saw him. "What do you need?" she said stonily.

He felt as if he had been slapped. Silvia was normally very cheerful—an important prerequisite for work at the town hall—always ready with a joke or a compliment, but now she just stood there with her arms folded and . . . and *looked* at him, no expression in her eyes. His voice shook as he asked for six half-pound packages of manna, a loaf of bread, and a quart of milk.

Silvia looked up his records on the computer, checked off that portion of his weekly allotment, and went to fetch his supplies, all without saying a word. She piled the supplies on the counter, then retreated to the back room. McFarland had forgotten the cloth bag he normally used for hauling food, so he scooped the packages awkwardly up in his arms, his heart poisoned with the beginnings of bitterness.

As McFarland reentered the foyer, Jed Thomas was just leaving the council chambers. The head councilman wore an angry expression on his round, pugnacious face; his coveralls were rumpled and he looked haggard, as if he had just woken up. "Good Lord, if it isn't Carl 'the Great Satan' McFarland," said Thomas. His voice carried an undertone of nastiness that McFarland didn't like at all. "You're the *last* person I hoped I'd run into today."

"That's fine, Jed. I'm just on my way home."

McFarland headed for the doors, but Thomas cut him off. "Slow down a second. I need to have a few words with you anyway."

McFarland sighed wearily and shifted his supplies into a more comfortable position. His shoulders and elbows were beginning to get sore now, too. James Ivie, still rocked back on his chair, discreetly pretended he wasn't there. "Make it quick," said McFarland. "I've got a lot to do this afternoon."

"I sure hope it doesn't involve cooking up ways to spoil the revival tonight," said Thomas, planting his fists on his hips.

McFarland, no longer tall himself, still had a good six inches on Thomas, and he glared down at the man with as much forcefulness as he could muster. "I don't believe what I do with my afternoon is any of your business."

"It is if it threatens the well-being of this community." The tips of Thomas's ears burned red. "Dammit to hell, Carl, I spent half the night closeted in there with that pastor and two of his flunkies, trying to convince them that this town is *righteous* enough to be allowed to benefit from their technology. If you pull any stunts tonight like you did last night, they're liable to just pack up and leave us sitting here with our peters in our pockets!"

"I seriously doubt that, Jed. They're just trying to keep you off-balance so you don't figure out what they're really up to until its too late for you to do anything about it. They're playing you for a patsy."

"I'm giving the perimeter guards orders not to let you near that tent tonight." Thomas jabbed McFarland in the chest to punctuate his words. Then he seemed to soften a bit. "Carl, this town owes a lot to you, probably its entire existence. But in case you didn't notice, you're *old* now. You can't still play the hero. You're not the most popular man in town at the moment. I'd hate to see you get hurt or anything." He started for the front doors.

"If that's a threat, it's a pretty wimpy one," said McFarland. Thomas halted with the door half-open, and frigid air swirled in. "By the way, Jed, you wouldn't happen to be the one who let those folks have Martha Stillman's body yesterday, would you?"

Thomas said nothing, just stared outside with his nostrils flared.

"You might want to just pop down to Winnemucca Street and pay a visit on the Stillmans. I'm sure they'd love to see you." McFarland let his voice fall into a sneer. "When you get back, you *tell* me those churchies mean this town any good."

The door slammed shut behind Thomas.

A hand on his shoulder startled McFarland. "Here," said Ivie. He was balanced on his crutch and his one good leg, an old fleece-lined jacket draped over his arm. "You'll probably want this on your way home."

McFarland started to protest, then thought better of it. Ivie was a good man, and persistent. When the plague tide had crept up on him as he was gathering manna, he had not panicked, but had hopped back to safety while the voracious nanomachines devoured his lower leg, and he had done his best to spray himself with water from his tank as he went. Only when he was certain he was free of plague did he cross the moat and allow himself to collapse. The heat released by the breaking of molecular bonds in his leg had been sufficient to cauterize the stump, which probably saved his life.

It was that same cauterizing action, however, that had meant death for—for—

"Thank you," said McFarland, pushing away the painful thought. He knew that a man like Ivie wouldn't be put off without a long and exhausting argument, and all his combative feelings were draining away. He let the man help him shrug into the jacket.

"Just bring that back by, next time you pick up your allotment," said Ivie, hobbling back to his chair. "Oh, by the way, Carl, you haven't seen my daughter today, have you? She was going to come by here with some lunch."

"She was at my place earlier for science class," said McFarland, "but then she left for that Bible workshop." He had to juggle his packages as he tried to work the snaps up the front of the jacket. "That was an hour or two ago. But she's a good girl. It's probably just the weather holding her up."

"If you see her, would you give her a gentle reminder that her father is stuck here starving?" said Ivie with a smile, lowering himself into his chair.

Dammit, thought McFarland as he headed back into the wind, warm in the borrowed jacket, indefinable guilt trickling fresh over his heart. Just when I think I can give up on this town . . .

4

Only isolated drops of rain spattered the ground as the storm swept over town. The clouds roiled and scudded overhead without releasing their precious store of water. McFarland had been hoping for a downpour; it would have made things much easier for him that night, besides benefiting Wellington by staving off the plague tide for twenty-four hours. The townspeople could have gathered all the manna they could carry, free of cumbersome water tanks and of the fear of having an accident like James Ivie's.

McFarland was hiking back up the ridge to his house, leaning into the strengthening wind, when he heard shouts from off to his right, down by the river. The cries were faint, whipped away by the wind. He hurried off the path and into the trees, hugging his food to his chest, until he emerged at a point that overlooked the river from high up. Below, the river crooked sharply to the north, away from him, then turned lazily back to the east perhaps eighty yards further on. Fir trees marched in profusion down the side of the ridge, but the growth ended abruptly at a line twenty yards from the river. The trees had been stripped away here for greater protection from the plague and easier monitoring by the perimeter guards. Beyond the river was only a undulating silver landscape, punctuated at irregular intervals by dots that were either packaged tofu or guns and ammunition.

One of those guards was spraying water at a scintillating patch of silver spreading across the sand halfway between the river and the trees. He was pumping furiously with his right hand, aiming the nozzle with his left, but he was spraying into the wind, and much of his water was blown straight back at him. He couldn't circle around and attack from the leeward, however, because the wind might carry the plague straight into the trees, where it would be next to impossible to rout out. Instead, his own body would catch whatever particles of plague might lose their molecular grip on the sand in the next strong gust.

McFarland, helpless on the ridge, heard the man's faraway shouts, felt his own heart racing faster, watched as the silvery patch expanded. Why, the guard was really no more than a boy, perhaps Orrin's age or a bit older. McFarland's eyes misted. The boy would give his life for the community if he had to, ransom all the years left ahead of him in exchange for the lives of his fellows. And not even such a sacrifice would guarantee Wellington's survival.

What sort of community could make these kinds of demands on its young?

"One I helped create," McFarland whispered to himself. He realized belatedly that his clenched hands were mashing the packages of manna out of shape.

Another perimeter guard rounded the treeline at the river's far bend at a run, and McFarland turned away from the scene. He felt dizzy, and he labored to control his breathing. The boy would be all right. Help was coming, and together the two guards would contain the plague, wash it down into the river.

But in his inability to help, McFarland felt the stirrings of a new and unfamiliar kind of guilt. What right had he to exist in relative comfort and leisure, while boys and girls risked their young lives to protect him?

But you've done your duty by this town, he told himself as he hiked the rest of the way back to his house. You've done your best, you've given your all. Jed Thomas is right: you're *old*, and the best thing you can do for the community now is to stay out of the way while younger, nimbler hands do what needs to be done, while younger, nimbler minds chart out Wellington's future.

But something inside him hollered, "Bullshit!"

After all, who was the one who first recognized the threat of the plague when it materialized from out of the desert forty years before? Who was it that led the town's defense, rallying the community, getting the citizens to turn on their hoses, their sprinklers, their irrigation systems to hold back the silvery tide? Whose idea was it to dig a moat so the river would effectively encircle the town, protection against the eventual failure of the water mains? Who had designed the wind turbines and supervised their installation? Who had determined that all radio transmitters must be done away with? Who had developed the system of pumps and electrical heaters that kept a trickle of water circulating through the riverbeds even in winter? Who had established the protocols for gathering food, standing watch over the moat, disposing of human waste and of human dead?

Dammit, who was it that *saved* this ridiculous little town?

McFarland stopped to rest against a tree, his supplies still cradled in his arms, within sight of the line of stones that marked his property. The wind screamed and howled all around him, and a single mocking drop of rain hit him on the forehead. He remembered the confusion and panic in Wellington the day the plague made its first appearance, spreading across the horizon out of the eastern desert. It was the day of his father's funeral, and McFarland, with as little faith as he put in religion, had still managed to convince himself that the plague was a sign from beyond the grave—a sign of Pastor McFarland's displeasure with his only begotten son. Greg Winder, an old high school friend, had come barreling down State Road 208 from Yerington in his battered Toyota four-by-four. He fishtailed to a stop on the cemetery lawn—disrupting the burial and nearly running down Eileen and Hillary—and stumbled down from the cab raving about a sea of mercury out in the desert that swallowed up rocks and plants and people and cars and houses whole.

Within the hour, the plague was visible from Wellington.

It was no use fleeing to the east; the entire desert landscape was coated with silver. Those who tried to flee up U.S. 395 to Lake Tahoe were stopped by a wave of plague sweeping down the Sierras from the northwest, and those who fled south into the Toiyabe National Forest were blocked before they reached Bridgeport by another front boiling up from California.

That had been the beginning.

No one knew how the plague had originated. The television and radio stations from Reno and Vegas and Sacramento had fallen silent after giving only spotty reports of destruction from all around the region. McFarland recognized the fruits of Project Scorched Earth, of course, but that didn't tell him how it had escaped, or whether it had perhaps been stolen by or sold to the agent of some foreign power. His earliest speculations were that it may have gotten loose from the Dugway Proving Grounds in western Utah, or from some other desert testing center, but it had appeared too suddenly in too many different places to be explained that way. Perhaps it had been delivered to dozens of locations simultaneously by a legion of suicidal terrorists, or by an insurgent cabal from within the military itself, or released into the atmosphere to waft to earth by foreign planes.

Whatever the explanation, the United States had been wiped out, and probably all of North America. Maybe the plague had crossed the Panama Canal by now, or the Bering Strait. Planes had been spotted overhead only twice; on the second occasion Connor Jewett, a former pilot, had his binoculars ready, and he claimed the aircraft were European Community reconnaissance jets.

Thirty-five years had passed without another sign of the outside world.

McFarland had often wondered, chilled, if there were anything left of the outside world at all.

It was obvious now that there was. It was also obvious that somewhere some government laboratory had survived the plague, or had at least retained its integrity. Somewhere, that charlatan of an old-time revivalist had managed to dig up the plague's counteragent, and to ferret out what was left of Project Rapture. McFarland imagined he was using them to build up some kind of quasi-religious empire from the ruins of North America, an empire based on fear and false miracles rather than the honest values of faith and decency.

So who was better qualified to confront the threat than the one man who understood it?

No one!

McFarland pushed himself off from the tree against which he was resting, an expression of grim determination on his face. And bullshit to whomever said he was too old!

When he reached his house, he dropped the manna and the bread on the kitchen counter, used a flint striker to light a candle made from sheep tallow, and carried the container of milk down to the basement. It was the coolest place in the house, and here the milk would be slower to go sour. He didn't worry about preserving the manna; it would stay good for years, and it even came in its own olive-drab plastic packaging, with a label that read: "Combat Meal, Individual, Nutritionally Complete."

Shadows capered like demons in the corners of what had once been a well-appointed rec room, and the smell of rot from the carpeting and the old hide-a-bed was heavy. McFarland set the glass container of milk on a low table. He had never really liked goats' milk, particularly when it was warm, but there had been no cows inside the town's defensive perimeter when the plague struck. There were two empty milk bottles nearby; he kept forgetting to take them back. Someone from the storehouse would be up here soon looking for him. He smiled wryly at the thought of Silvia Gonsalves crashing through his front door like Arnold Schwarzenegger in one of the *Terminator* movies of his childhood, demanding he return his empties.

Holding the candle high, he moved around the bar at the far end of the room. Taphandles that had never let flow any drink harder than tonic water or root beer threw shadows like tall, marching soldiers in the orange light. McFarland knelt almost reverently behind the bar, setting the candle down on the damp carpet. This was a pilgrimage of sorts, to earlier, simpler, if not happier, times. As a child, he had hidden in these cabinets on many occasions to eavesdrop as his father heard confessions and dispensed advice to the various members of his flock. He had never been caught, and he considered that one of the few true miracles of his life.

His father had seemed as wise as Solomon in those hours, using his easy manner and gentle tongue to cut to the essence of whatever problem he was presented with, and as McFarland

knelt there behind the bar the ghosts of those long-ago conver-
sations seemed to settle about his shoulders like a cloak of dust.
Pastor McFarland had had good advice and kind words aplenty
for everyone—everyone with the exception of his only son—but
during those magical hours young Carl had been able to share in
his father's wisdom and love, had been able to imagine that he,
too, was important in the eyes of the God his father served, had
been able to forget that his only real role in life was that of an
example, an object lesson, a preacher's son.

McFarland tugged on the handle of the miniature refrigerator
nestled beneath the bar. He had only disturbed this cache once
in the time since his father's death. The magnetic seal around the
door was falling apart, but the hinges were rusting so badly that
the door made grating and groaning noises as he forced it open.
To McFarland's ears, it was the sound of a dying man's death
rattle. The flickering light revealed a large stoppered flask inside,
standing upright in a special rack, and two syringelike devices
wrapped in clear plastic.

He withdrew the syringes and then the flask, which contained a cloudy solution resembling dilute semen. He nodded to
himself. It seemed fitting, in this place where his father seemed
almost to live again, to have hidden the means by which his
body could have been restored to a semblance of life.

This was the sacrament of Project Rapture.

Just over forty years had passed since McFarland had smug-
gled the flask out of the laboratories at MIT. He had left Wellington, left *home*, at the age of seventeen, as soon as he had his
high-school diploma in hand. He attended Berkeley on scholar-
ship, went on to graduate studies at MIT, but never once had he
returned home—until at the age of forty he received word of his
father's death.

The news stunned him. McFarland knew his departure had hurt his father deeply, but he had always intended to return someday, sit down with his father man-to-man and hash out their differences, make up for his long years of silence. Somehow, though, the right opportunity had never come up. McFarland had always respected the wisdom his father showed in those meetings with his parishioners, but now that the man was dead, the sick ache inside him, the unquenchable yearning, told him that he had actually loved his father, too.

All he wanted was a chance to tell him that—as if the simple words "I love you, Dad" could erase all the years of bitterness and recrimination that had passed. In his grief, McFarland had stolen the Rapture solution, convinced that at the wake or at the funeral or sometime in between he would be able to inject the body, tell his father those four magic words, and beg his forgiveness for all the pain and anger that ran between them.

But McFarland hadn't had the courage—or the recklessness— to go through with it. Once a body was revived from death, it wasn't so easy to put it back there again. His father might be angry at the early resurrection, might refuse to forgive him, might try to send him to his room or inflict some other childhood punishment on his forty-year-old physicist son. And what's more, McFarland knew he would deserve whatever he got . . .

So as they lowered the mahogany casket into the ground, McFarland's last goodbyes to his father remained unspoken. The first spadeful of dirt was barely thrown before Greg Winder screeched into the parking lot, bouncing up over the curb and onto the grass, and after that, McFarland and his wife and small daughter knew no world but the tiny enclosure that was Wellington, Nevada. He had kept himself free for twenty-three years, but in the end his father had trapped him there for good.

Of course, McFarland no longer saw it that way. His father's death had no doubt saved his life and the lives of Eileen and Hillary . . . but kneeling there behind the bar, a place so rich in memories and guilt, it was difficult to separate the way he felt now from the way he had felt growing up, and the way he had felt upon returning to Wellington. McFarland shoved the two syringes into the pocket of his overalls and pushed himself to his feet, knees creaking dangerously. With only candlelight for a guide, he climbed out of the dank basement and back into the world of the present.

In the kitchen, he held the flask up to the light, then swirled it gently. The cloudiness turned into a faint pinkish glow, which meant the suspended nanomachines were still active even after forty years. Good. The longer they were exposed to light, even the thin light of the passing storm, the more energy they would absorb and the richer the red would become.

His emergency water tank leaned against the wall. McFarland checked that it was full, then tested the straps and the nozzle to make sure they were in working order. When he was satisfied with the condition of the tank, he opened the pantry and from the top shelf took down a dark gray pistol wrapped in cloth, along with a fully loaded magazine.

The gun and shells were products of the plague, lightweight and superstrong, assembled one molecule at a time from pure carbon. The powder was a mixture of potassium nitrate, sulfur, and carbon in the form of charcoal, which were all easily synthesized from chemical building blocks available in the local soil, and the interior of the barrel was protected by a thin layer of carbon steel. Left out in the plague tide, the pistol would have been broken down into its constituent molecules for recycling three days after its creation. McFarland had rescued it from that fate a few weeks earlier. He always liked to keep a fresh pistol on hand, though he had never before found reason to use one.

He clicked the magazine into the grip and slipped the pistol into the pocket of his overalls. Then he opened a package of manna, tore off a chunk of bread, and sat down at the kitchen table eat, and to wait. When the solution had darkened to the color of blood, he would fill the syringes. As darkness approached, he would strap on the tank and be on his way.

If he happened to be watching, McFarland hoped his father would forgive him for what he was about to do.

5

"And this same Nicodemus," cried the reverberating voice of the preacher, "a ruler of the Jews, a Pharisee, a member of the very sect that persecuted our Lord Christ Jesus and tried to trap him in his words that they might have cause to prosecute him at the law—he, even *he*, came to Jesus in the night and said unto him, 'Rabbi, we know that thou art a teacher come from God: for no man can do these miracles that thou doest, except God be with him.'"

McFarland rolled stiffly under the edge of the revival tent. He lay in the dirt for a moment, dizzy, the words of the preacher buffeting him like waves eroding a rocky shore. He was behind the platform, and he could see the network of metal struts that supported it. He could also see the heavy black curtain that hung to the floor from the front of the platform, hiding the supports from the view of the audience. He stood up carefully, his joints screaming as if all their cartilage had disintegrated, staying hunched over so his head was below the level of the platform. The legs of his overalls were wet from the knees down, and little flecks of mud clung to him from the moist ring of condensation drippings that encircled the tent.

From behind, the preacher was a dark blot in the blinding floodlights, gesturing, pacing back and forth like a caged animal. "Now, this could not have been any easy thing for Nicodemus to admit. His peers, his closest associates, his *friends*, were hatching a frenzy of schemes to discredit this Christ, this Redeemer, this self-proclaimed Messiah whose coming had been prophesied for four thousand *years*. But when a man, or a woman, or a child, witnesses the kinds of miracles that Nicodemus had seen Christ perform, only the willing blindness of his eyes, the deafness of his ears, the hardness of his heart, can keep him from feeling the Spirit of Truth which whispers to his soul, which testifies that such things are possible only through the goodness, the mercy, and the power of Almighty *God!*"

About ten yards to McFarland's right, centered behind the platform, was a narrow set of rollaway stairs, its casters blocked with chunks of wood. He headed toward it, checking his pockets to make sure he hadn't dropped the gun or the syringes. Just after sunset he had crossed the man-made section of the moat south of his ridge, then traveled through the desert in a wide half-circle, spraying himself a safe corridor, until in full darkness he reached the portion of the perimeter that Orrin was guarding. He had left his cumbersome water tank in the canal as Orrin helped him climb up onto unpolluted soil; if things went well tonight, McFarland would be able to stroll home right through the center of town, with no fear that cronies of Jed Thomas might so much as lay a finger on him. The townspeople would have the technology they needed to really fight off the plague tide, and their lives could begin to return to normal.

"Nicodemus asked no question aloud," said the preacher, "but the Lord could see into his heart, could read the unspoken question that was written there as easily as you or I can read a book.

The question that consumed this Pharisee to the point that he would risk his living, his social standing, his very position in the community to have it answered, was this: How may a man see the kingdom of God? And Jesus answered this question, saying, 'Verily, verily, I say unto thee, except a man be born again, he cannot see the kingdom of God.'"

McFarland had reached the base of the stairs when a hand clapped him on the shoulder. "Is this our old unbeliever friend from last night?" said a voice that sounded both threatening and amused.

As McFarland turned he fumbled for the gun in his pocket. The man behind him, however, seized McFarland's wrist in an iron grip and spun him around. McFarland gasped as his bones ground together. The man who held him was a churchie, tall, with bristly blond hair, a square jaw, and glazed-over sky-blue eyes. He looked so Aryan that McFarland could only think of him as "Adolf." "*Montezuma!*" hissed McFarland, his teeth gritted against the pain.

Adolf only laughed. His eyes did not change, nor did they move. "A rather silly magic word, don't you think?" he said, smiling in a friendly way. "I, for one, am happy to have been re-conditioned."

McFarland, dazed with pain, almost found himself nodding. The Army colonel who had selected the keywords that tripped a revivified corpse into and out of unquestioning obedience, had been taking a subtle poke at the Marine Corps, whom he referred to as a "pack of jarheaded zombies." But the pain in his wrist swelled suddenly; black spots swarmed before his eyes, and his head rolled back.

"We didn't know if you were going to be back tonight," said Adolf, "but Pastor Smith really hoped you would be. You're such an effective foil, it makes his case all the stronger." He reached into McFarland's pocket and removed the pistol. "Let me relieve you of this, and then you can carry on with your business. You can't stop God's work, but you can certainly help move it forward." He spun McFarland back around and gave him a push toward the stairs. McFarland tripped, hitting his knees on the lowest step and cutting his outthrust palms on the ragged metal edge of another. "Go on. Your public is waiting."

Shaking, McFarland pushed himself to his feet. The stairs seemed to sway, and he felt sick in the pit of his stomach. I need some Dramamine, he thought crazily, then started up the stairs, leaning too heavily for safety's sake against the flimsy metal railing.

He heard Adolf's soft laughter behind him.

The preacher's diatribe was barreling ahead under full steam. "Now, Nicodemus, certainly taken aback by the Lord's perception of the things in his heart, by this fresh proof that Jesus was indeed a man of power, asked, 'How can a man be born when he is old? Can he enter the second time into his mother's womb, and be born?'

"And Jesus answered, 'Verily, verily, I say unto thee, except a man be born of water and of the Spirit, he cannot enter into the kingdom of God.'

"Now, my dear, dear brothers and sisters in Christ, we have all been born of water. We have floated safe and secure in the life-giving waters of our mothers' wombs until our strength was such that it could no longer be contained, and we *pushed* our way out into this world. I say unto you, this is the first birth of which Jesus spoke, the birth by water! But there is of necessity a *second* birth, a cleansing by fire and by the Holy Ghost, without which—"

McFarland had by now mounted the platform, and a murmur rippled through the crowd. The lights all around were white-hot and blinding, but in the darkness beyond he could see that the crowd was much larger than it had been the night before. The sides of the tent bellied out beyond its capacity; there was no room in the aisles to walk. Every person in town but the perimeter guards and firemen must have been there. The murmuring swelled, and members of the audience began to point.

The preacher turned. When he saw McFarland his eyes narrowed with hatred, but his mouth curved into a smile. Sweat poured down the sides of his face, and a red, chafed line ran around his neck, just above the stiff black clerical collar. "Ah, Brother McFarland!" he said, holding out a comradely arm. "Come join us, please! We were just discussing the second birth, the baptism by fire! You are just in time, perhaps, to assist with a small demonstration!"

Ice filled McFarland's gut, and the platform seemed to reel like a raft. In the scenario he had envisioned, all the backstage guards would have been subdued by now, enslaved by the mystic word *"Montezuma!"*, and he would now draw his pistol and shoot the preacher, careful not to damage the brain or the heart. Once the man's life had ebbed away, McFarland would inject him with the Rapture solution, demonstrating to the gathered crowd how *anyone* could perform a miracle, if they only possessed the right technology.

But now he was trapped. Stupid, deluded old fool! Did he really believe that an eighty-year-old man could pull off such Indiana Jones-style derring-do?

He heard Adolf's slow footsteps on the stair behind him, and he moved forward.

Hundreds of jeers and catcalls arose from the crowd, not all of them fit for what was putatively a worship service. "Please, please!" said the preacher, turning back to the audience. "We are gathered here in God's name! Let us not poison the spiritual atmosphere with such ugliness and filth! Despite his unbelief, Brother McFarland is still a child of God! Let us treat him so, that perhaps our love and united good feelings will suffice to convert him from ignorance and blindness unto light and life everlasting!"

"Yeah, right," McFarland muttered angrily. Sweat from his armpits trickled down his ribs, but the rage he felt at his own stupidity helped to steady his stomach and his vision.

The preacher put his arm around him, and McFarland shuddered as he would at the touch of a snake. The man smelled of musk, and there was mint on his breath. "Last night," said the preacher, "one of your fellow townswomen rose up from the dead on this very stage. Do you remember that?"

"I do," said McFarland, inclining his head toward the preacher's hidden microphone. He felt like a contestant on a television game show.

"Those who were with us last night will recall the event as a miraculous outpouring of God's love and mercy, a quickening by fire and by the Holy Spirit, indeed, the very second birth of which Christ spoke to Nicodemus more than two thousand years ago! Our blessed and well-beloved sister Martha Stillman is now *assured* of life eternal in the mansions of our all-powerful Lord and Master! Praise be to God!"

"Hallelujah!" shouted scores of voices, and McFarland could have sworn he heard June Burlingame's nasal whine among them.

The preacher gave McFarland's shoulders a brotherly squeeze. "This day, God in his infinite mercy has marked out *more* of our brothers and sisters here in Wellington to taste of the sweet fruits of everlasting life!"

McFarland felt the ice in his stomach spread out into his veins. He's going to kill me, he thought. He's going to kill me and then bring my body back to life! He glanced behind him, but saw Adolf and another man and a woman standing guard at the rear of the platform. There was no place for him to run.

The preacher raised his free arm as if to embrace the entire crowd and shouted, "Bring forth the fallen!"

The tent flaps parted behind the crowd, and six young churchies entered, bearing a white-shrouded body on their shoulders. The crowd parted to let them through. Then another six entered bearing another body, and another six, and another, until there were seven bodies being borne down the center aisle in all, and the tent flaps closed again behind them.

A strange calmness descended over McFarland, and he suppressed the grim smile that touched his lips. He wasn't going to die after all—and there might still be a way for him to come out of this mess on top.

The procession turned right when it reached the head of the aisle, then mounted a set of stairs positioned at the far end of the platform. In a few moments the seven bodies were laid out in a neat row, shoulder to shoulder, and the bearers had dispersed into the crowd.

The preacher released McFarland and went to the far end of the row of bodies. McFarland, at the opposite end, took a few steps back, to where he could see both the preacher and the crowd. The preacher knelt and, with a grand flourish, whipped the shroud from off the first body. It settled to the stage behind him, like a streamer of white frosting applied carelessly to a cake. The preacher looked up at McFarland, his beard bristling. "You claim to be a man of science, do you not, Brother McFarland? Knowledgeable in the ways of medicine and biology?"

"I was trained as a physicist, not as a doctor," said McFarland irritably. He was trying to identify the man who had just been uncovered.

"Well," said the preacher with a laugh, "surely your familiarity with the medical sciences is sufficient to allow you to pronounce this brother of ours either dead or alive, is it not? For the benefit of any doubters among us?"

McFarland frowned, then crossed behind the row of shrouds and knelt. He recognized the corpse now as Dale Bradley, a man of about twenty-five whom he had not known well. He felt Bradley's throat for a pulse, lifted the man's eyelids and peered into his pupils, placed his cheek beside the mouth and felt for breath. After making a great show, he stood again and said, "The *cause* isn't immediately apparent, but as far as I can tell, this man is certainly dead."

"Dead!" cried the preacher, rising to whirl upon the audience. "*Dead*, do you hear? Dead to the things of this world! Dead to *sin*, even as Paul wrote unto the Romans! 'They that are in the flesh cannot please God,' he told them! 'How shall we, that are dead to sin, live any longer therein? Know ye not, that so many of us as were baptized into Jesus Christ were baptized into his *death?*' "

The preacher moved back and forth across the stage like a dervish, shaking a hand at the crowd and emphasizing his points by pounding his fist into an open palm. " 'Ye are not in the flesh, but in the *Spirit*, if it so be that the Spirit of God dwell in you! And if *Christ* be in you, the body is *dead* because of sin! Therefore we are *buried* with him by *baptism* into death: that like as *Christ* was raised up from the dead by the glory of the Father, even so *we also* should walk in *newness* of *life!*' "

Then he flung himself to his knees beside the body of Dale Bradley, clapped a hand to either side of the man's neck, and cried,

"Now awake, o thou that in Christ art dead to sin, and *arise!*"

The body jerked suddenly, as if shocked by electricity, and its eyes opened. As the preacher withdrew his hands, McFarland caught a glimpse of a thin, flesh-colored tube running down the man's palm and into the sleeve of his jacket from a ring on his finger. Then Dale Bradley blinked and slowly sat up, looking around himself like a man just roused from a long nap. The preacher stood and offered Bradley his hand, then helped the man to his feet. Bradley's head moved from side to side. "Where is this?" he said in a flat tone of voice.

"You're still in Wellington, my friend, your home," said the preacher. "Can you tell us your name?"

The man knew what he was doing, McFarland had to admit. Getting a reanimated corpse to speak its name was a vital part of the reawakening process. It helped to reestablish identity, reopen dormant pathways in the cerebral cortex. It enabled the subject to know himself, and to stave off the panic of partial amnesia.

Bradley turned his gaze toward the preacher—but only partway, McFarland noted. "I am Dale Fenton Bradley. I somehow had the idea that I was dead. Am I dead?"

The preacher laughed joyfully. "You were dead, but now you are reborn, Brother Bradley! You have been numbered among the children of the Lamb, and the sweetness of eternal life is yours! Let us sing hosannas to the name of Almighty God!"

Hundreds of voices chorused in praise. McFarland thought he might be able to shut them up by asking Bradley if he remembered how he had *come* to be dead, but forbore. There would be a much more effective way to put his point across, if only he was patient . . .

As the voices quieted, the preacher said, "Are your loved ones here with us tonight, Brother Bradley? Your family?"

"I have no family," said Bradley almost abstractedly, gazing off into nothingness. "My father and mother have been dead for many years ago. It is only I."

"It is *not* only you," said the preacher, sweeping his arm in gesture that took in everyone in the tent. "This is your family now, dear brother! *We* are your family, as well as your mother and father, who I am sure are here with us tonight. Did you not see them, Brother Bradley, in the hours when you were dead as to the flesh? Did they not visit you, clothed in radiance, and converse with you, and did they not send you back to us that you might be delivered of your second birth?"

"My mother and father . . . ? I saw them . . . ?"

These were not entirely questions, but they were not entirely statements, either. Not that it'll matter to this crowd, thought McFarland. That's all the proof of the existence of an afterlife they'll ever need—the word of a confused and highly suggestible revivified corpse.

The preacher led the crowd in more hallelujahs, and when they had quieted down he turned to McFarland, keeping a hand on Bradley's shoulder. "Those of us who were in attendance at this great meeting last evening heard you give a marvelous—and, I might add, completely fanciful—explanation of the plague which so thoroughly besets us, in terms of that scientific knowledge which you hold so dear. Much to our misfortune, however, you were so overcome by the Spirit that you could not maintain consciousness long enough to provide a similar explanation for the quickening of the mortal remains of Martha Stillman." His eyes narrowed. "You *do* have such an explanation, I presume?"

"I do," said McFarland, keeping his voice steady despite the anger that trembled inside him.

"Then I challenge you to do so now, my friend, for the edification of all present! Tell us in your"—his nose seemed to wrinkle—"*scientific* terms how it is possible that our beloved Brother Bradley walks again among the living! I *defy* you to make a case for yourself!"

The preacher had turned Dale Bradley until the young man faced in McFarland's direction. The empty eyes seemed fixed on a point somewhere above McFarland's head. McFarland shuddered, disconcerted, but his voice quavered only a bit as he said, "I'll go you one better than. I'll show you how it's done!"

He knelt then, and flipped the shroud away from the second body in the row.

The first thing that registered on McFarland was the beauty of the long red hair. The second was the whiteness of the skin, the blueness of the lips. The third was the liberal application of theatrical powder around the throat and neck, imperfectly obscuring two lines of oval bruises.

It was a moment before McFarland's numbed mind could correlate all these items and put a name to them.

Rachel Ivie.

A sudden upwelling of grief closed off his throat, and shame burned behind his eyes. This was his own fault, his alone. He had driven her out of his house that morning with that damned sharp tongue of his . . .

But he couldn't afford to show any emotion, any hesitation. Like an illusionist, whatever hold he might exert over the audience would disappear with the first interruption to the flow of his actions. If he moved on to the next body in the row, his advantage would be gone. And the preacher or one of his minions might have time to put a stop to McFarland's counterdemonstration. Forgive me, Rachel, he said silently as he drew the two syringes from the pocket of his overalls. Forgive me for desecrating this body.

Forgive me for everything.

Each syringe ended in a ring of twelve short needles. McFarland discarded the plastic cap that protected each ring of needles, then held the syringes high. The Rapture solution gleamed like dark blood inside the clear plastic. "These syringes are loaded with a solution of nanomachines I helped develop for the Army more than forty years ago," he said loudly, as if lecturing to a huge freshman biology class. "Their object was to create a practically indestructible soldier, by reviving the dead bodies on a battlefield."

He swung his arms through opposing arcs and stabbed the short needles into both sides of Rachel's neck. As he slowly depressed the plungers, he felt warmth in the corners of his eyes and a hard knot in his throat. "These nanomachines fan out through the body under their own power," he said, struggling to keep the emotion out of his voice, "each targeted to a specific location and tissue type. Some will strengthen and knit together muscle fibers, providing a pathway for the electrical impulses that cause our muscles to contract. Some will take over the functions of the blood in carrying oxygen to cells and then carrying wastes away. Still other will enter the brain to reestablish and provide electrical stimulus to the neural pathways that have been decaying since the time of death. All are replicating themselves from the body's own raw materials."

McFarland looked out over the audience. "And in case you're wondering, we *did* try this out on a few live subjects once. Volunteers." He gave a thin smile. "They went crazy. Turned into gibbering lunatics, actually. You see, only dead people can cope with having their brains invaded by nanomachines—because they're not around to feel it happen. That's why our friend the good preacher has to kill people before turning them into his slaves."

A gradual blush had returned to Rachel's cheeks, and McFarland bent over her once again. "Once all the nanomachines are in place, it takes only a loud noise to stimulate the reticular formation, a nerve net in the brainstem that regulates our level of awareness, into wakefulness." McFarland clapped his hands together hard, barking out a short *"Hah!"* The body jerked, and the lovely green eyes fluttered open. Several members of the crowd jumped as well, startled. "This signals the nanomachines in the cardiac tissue to deliver enough of an electric shock to the heart to start it beating again—and, for all practical purposes, the body lives again. Only a direct and massive injury to the heart or brain will shut down bodily functions again."

"Carl?" said Rachel sleepily, her voice rasping in a dry throat.

A gasp ran through the audience as McFarland helped her stand. The feel of her cold, smooth, trusting hand in his made his shame all the greater. She looked at the crowd through the bright floodlights without squinting, then looked at McFarland. Her hair was disarrayed, and her eyes, like a blind person's, didn't seem to register him. "What happened, Carl? I don't remember—"

A harsh cry erupted from near the middle of the audience. A man and woman were on their feet, struggling through the crowd toward the clogged center aisle. *"Rachel!"* cried the man. *"Rachel!"*

"Daddy . . . ?" said Rachel, turning her face to the crowd again.

McFarland tried to call out to Rachel's parents. "Mr. and Mrs. Ivie, your daughter is—"

"Enough!" shouted the preacher suddenly, stepping to front of

the platform. McFarland felt a sudden, sickening surety that the man had allowed the business with Rachel to proceed only as far as suited his needs. The preacher had watched the demonstration impassively, but now his face was red with righteous anger, and his amplified voice drowned out all other sound. "I will stand for this blasphemy no longer! I was willing to give you the benefit of doubt, Brother McFarland, to believe that you were a skeptical soul who yet sought honestly after truth, and who would recognize it when it was presented to him. But in this my hopes were misplaced! You bear the powers of the Adversary within you, yea, even the dark priesthood of Satan himself, who sends forth deceitful workers, false apostles, and who transforms even himself into an angel of light, that the children of men might be blinded and dragged down to *hell!*"

Rachel tugged on McFarland's hand. "Carl, is that my daddy? Why is everyone shouting?"

McFarland saw Ivie flailing through the crowd with only a crutch to clear his way, saw a dozen churchies converging on him and his wife from all directions. The sight of it tore his heart like a bullet. "If anyone here serves Satan, it's *you!*" he shouted back at the preacher, pain lending power to his voice. "You murder these innocent children, then bring them back to life to serve your own twisted ends! You're no better than a Cain or a Judas Iscariot!"

The preacher whirled on the audience. "Attend, my brothers and sisters! We know the Devil speaks words of flattery with a honeyed tongue! We know his servants possess the power to imitate the miracles of God! When Moses transformed his brother's staff into a serpent, did not Pharaoh order his magicians to do likewise? I say unto you that what you have witnessed here this night is no more than magician of Pharaoh turning his staff into a serpent!" His eyes burned like coals in the shadow of his clenched black brows. "But be not deceived! Whose was the greater power that day in Pharaoh's court? Why, *God's*, manifested through his prophet Moses—for Moses's serpent possessed strength enough to *devour* the serpents of the magicians!"

He seized Dale Bradley by the arm and hissed viciously into the man's ear, then propelled him toward McFarland and Rachel. Bradley's eyes glinted with a cold, hard light, and in his fist he gripped the haft of an ornamental dagger.

McFarland tried to shout, but strong arms seized him from behind and a hand clamped itself over his mouth.

"*Witness,*" roared the voice of the preacher, "*the devouring of Satan's serpent!*"

Rachel turned, uncomprehending, as Bradley raised the dagger high above his head. The crowd was in a frenzy, the Ivies' despairing cries lost in the general melee. McFarland twisted, bit at the hand covering his mouth, tried to shout instructions to Rachel, but she didn't hear. She only stared as the dagger descended.

It sank to the haft between her ribs, in the shallow concavity between her left breast and her sternum.

"*No!*" cried McFarland as Bradley withdrew the dagger. Rachel's body stiffened and began to topple. "*No!*"

The noise from the crowd was deafening.

There was a nasty laugh from behind him that he recognized as Adolf's. The hands loosened their grip, and McFarland surged forward, trying to catch Rachel as she fell, to spare her this one final indignity. Then he felt a hand shove him hard in the center of the back.

He collided with Rachel's body, and with his arms wrapped around her, her blood slicking the front of his overalls, they sprawled together off the front of the platform and into the crowd.

"*Witness the triumph of Almighty God!*" cried the preacher. "*Witness the power and glory of Christ's second birth! Tomorrow night, at the close of Easter Sunday, we offer this gift freely to all who wish to partake!*"

McFarland's face smashed against the top of someone's head. Blinding light flashed through his skull. Arms gathered him in, and he lost his purchase on Rachel's body. Faces swarmed crazily around him, tossing and rolling like a turbulent ocean, and then Jed Thomas was above him, staring down as he bobbed bloody and stunned in a cradle of strong arms.

"I *begged* you not to come tonight, Carl, I *swear* I did," said Thomas, grinning wickedly. "I guess you're just one of those people who only learns from hands-on experience."

A FRESH BREEZE CARESSED HIS FACE. HIS CHEEK RESTED AGAINST
soft grass, and he could smell the sweetness of morning dew. But
when he managed to pry open one of his blood- and sleep-en-
crusted eyelids, the first thing he thought of was winter.

He was staring up at the Sierras. The mountains were mantled in a
bone-white layer of snow that shaded gradually into silver plague the
farther down their slopes his eye traveled. And although the lower
portion of his vision was filled with grass and wildflowers and trees
and sunlit wind turbines and even a corner of his own snow-free
house, his brain insisted to him that it was still winter.

Still that *first* winter, in fact—that first snowfall—and if he
could get to the backyard fast enough, he could prevent the trag-
edy that was about to strike.

He pushed weakly at the ground. One hand screamed with
pain, as if it were broken, and he couldn't feel the other one at
all. He realized then that his right forearm was tucked beneath
his stomach, asleep. He tried to shift his weight, push himself up
with his left elbow, but the effort left his muscles trembling with
fatigue, and something sharp ground into him inside his chest.
He sank back to the ground.

"Carl . . . !"

His left eye snapped open again, and adrenaline flooded his veins. Eileen!

But after a moment of intense listening, his panic washed away, replaced by a bitter and familiar grief. Eileen was nearly forty years dead. He had fallen asleep for a moment, dreamed her voice.

His head nodded again.

"Daddeeeee . . . !"

This time McFarland made it almost to his knees before collapsing back to the grass. The right side of his chest was on fire. Tears of rage loosened the encrustations over his right eye. He wouldn't be able to slide back into sleep without hearing those voices again, those screams. God damn it all, he cried out inside. How could I have known there was any danger? How could I have known?

You knew every *other* damn thing about the plague, you sorry bastard.

But they never did any *tests* in the snow, not that *I* ever heard about!

His accusatory inner voice only laughed.

"Carl, please, oh my God, hurry, Carl . . . !"

McFarland jerked awake again, then collapsed in sobs. Bloody tears dripped into the grass.

The town had prepared so eagerly for the first snows. Everyone knew winter would offer them their best chance of escaping Wellington, with the entire landscape draped in a blanket of blessed frozen water. The townspeople laid in their supplies, readied cars and trucks to carry them over the mountains, into the desert, *anywhere* another center of life might be found. The need to locate and unite with other surviving communities was overwhelming. The urge to spread out beyond the prison of their crude moat was irresistible.

No one mentioned the possibility that the plague might respond differently to ice and snow than to liquid water.

The morning of the first snowfall, McFarland tramped all up and down the ridge making observations. As far as he could see, even up into the mountains and out across the desert, there was no evidence of plague. A uniform cloak of white shrouded everything within view. Satisfied, he started back toward the house.

Then he heard the screams, heard his name being shrieked out.

He ran, into the light wind sweeping down from the mountains. His borrowed boots and coat couldn't keep the cold out of his blood. When he reached the house and rounded the corner into the backyard, he skidded to a stop in the snow, and a sharp cry escaped him.

Two emaciated silvery figures clung together, writhing, in the snow. They more resembled products of Industrial Light & Magic than they did human beings. The larger figure was struggling to coat the smaller one with snow, but its hands and thin arms trembled too badly to do much good. At McFarland's cry, its head jerked up. Bits of blue iris shone through gaps in the silver that coated its withering eyes.

Eileen.

Later, after days of sleepless experimentation, McFarland was able to reconstruct what must happened in his backyard, *why* it had happened. The plague, he discovered, was inactivated only by contact with liquid water, and not by contact with ice. The presence of ice, however, alerted the nanomachines that free water might exist nearby, and they would swarm to the next non-threatening substance they came into contact with. It was a built-in survival mechanism—and a necessary one, if the plague was to have any efficacy on a snow-covered battlefield.

If no substance other than ice was present, the plague would carry out its regular program of molecular dismantling, reducing the crystalline H_2O to its component hydrogen and oxygen. This process released enough heat, however, to melt a tiny bit of the surrounding ice, which would in turn shut down some, but not all, of the nanomachines. The result was that the plague spread considerably more slowly in snow than on open ground, but it was also more difficult to detect. The best you could do was to keep your eyes open and avoid any mushy spots you might run across.

Plague in the snow was like a trap-door spider, just waiting for you to put your foot in its nest.

Judging by the footprints leading from the back door into the yard, five-year-old Hillary had been the first one to wander into the trap. McFarland could picture Eileen bundling her up in the borrowed snowsuit, then pushing her out the door to go play in the first snow. Perhaps Eileen had then gone to watch from the kitchen window. Perhaps she had seen it when Hillary stepped into the plague.

It would have engulfed the child within fifteen seconds, spreading not only beneath her clothes but into all the cavities of her body as well. Inactivated plague would coat her mucus membranes, with more swarming down her throat until her lungs were clogged. Her outer layer of skin would begin to dissolve, baring the nerve endings that lay underneath. She would only have had a short time when she was still able to scream.

Eileen's footprints were elongated and widely spaced. She had run to Hillary, tried to wash the child down with snow, but at her first touch the plague had engulfed her as well. At that point, there was no longer anything that could be done for either of them.

McFarland had shown up perhaps a minute later.

He reached for the emergency water tank they kept outside the back door, but the water had frozen and the tank had ruptured. He grabbed a shovel and came as close as he dared, then began heaving snow onto his wife and daughter in hopes that it might give them some relief. Eileen looked up with terrified eyes as the snow hit them, and McFarland's gut clenched at the idea that he was burying his family alive. She tried to reach out, tried to speak, but she couldn't get enough air. Her eyes were sunken, the sockets yawning wide. Hillary had already gone limp.

McFarland dropped the shovel and fled.

Work teams came up later to clear the yard of snow and to carry away what remained of the bodies. They carefully shoveled the infected snow into metal garbage cans, which were then heated until everything inside had melted. The garbage cans were then dumped and rinsed with clean water outside the moat. The bodies were placed outside the moat as well.

McFarland would have used the Rapture solution on them if he could have, but there wasn't enough left of their bodies to revive. As with his father before, he wanted to beg their forgiveness for running away, but he would never be able to. His subsequent frantic days of experimentation were only a refuge from the fact that he had failed his family when they needed him most—failed to protect them when he should have, and then failed to die with them when he should have. He cooked up scheme after scheme for killing himself, but he lacked the courage to actually go through with any of them. And besides, the town still needed him. If he couldn't protect his own family, at least he could try to protect the rest of the town.

McFarland raised his head and forced open both tired eyes. It wasn't winter after all. It really *was* spring. Eileen and Hillary had been gone for nearly forty years. He tried to picture them both in his mind, but what he came up with was something in between, an amalgam of childhood and adulthood, innocence and experience, naïveté and maturity. A lovely, smooth face with bright green eyes and beautiful long red hair . . .

Rachel. Oh God.

He heaved himself into a sitting position. Brilliant pain shot through his ribs, and pins and needles struck as the feeling began to return to his right arm. His left hand was bruised and misshapen; the fingers wouldn't close. Vaguely he remembered someone stomping on it. His stomach ached, and as he blinked around he spotted a thin pool of vomit drying a few yards farther up the slope of his lawn. There were black smears above him on the grass where he had rolled a ways down the hill, bleeding.

The sun was high in the cloudless eastern sky, and the wind off the mountains was cool. McFarland tried to stand up, but his head throbbed too badly. His memory of the previous night was beginning to come back. He would rather have had it stay forgotten. "This is the last warning you're going to get, old man," Jed Thomas had said, and his gang had carried McFarland up to the ridge and then thoroughly worked him over. "The only reason we don't kill you is out of courtesy for the fact that you used to be a town hero. *Used* to be. Remember that."

What McFarland would remember was the feel of his nose bursting under the impact of a thick fist. He felt it gingerly; it was soft and mushy, like plague-infected snow. Just what he deserved after what had happened to Rachel, what had happened to Hillary and Eileen. Thomas and his boys *should* have killed him. *That* would have been justice . . .

"Carl?" called a distant male voice, the sound echoing up the side of the ridge. "Carl, are you home?"

McFarland's head turned. The voice was real. He recognized it, but it was somehow subtly wrong. "Orrin?" he called back. His throat was sore from lying out in the cold all night, and his voice came out in a croak.

"Yes, Carl, it's me." Orrin crested the ridge a few moments later, walking surefootedly but not seeming to watch the path. McFarland realized why in the same instant that he realized what was wrong with Orrin's voice. There was no stutter.

"Oh, God, Orrin, they got you, too, didn't they?" McFarland closed his eyes, and tears bathed his cheeks. He felt like slumping back to ground and giving in to the pain in defeat.

Orrin's gangly figure loomed above him. McFarland couldn't see him well against the glare of the sun. He didn't speak for a few moments, and the wind blew around them both. The few birds that had survived the winter sang forlornly in the trees. "You're hurt," said Orrin at last, looking off toward the mountains.

McFarland drew his legs up, and his hands hung loosely between his knees. The dull ache from his left hand seemed to come from a million miles away; his half-numb right hand didn't even seem to be part of him. The only sharpness he felt was in his ribs. "Why don't you just kill me and get it over with?" he said. "That's what they sent you here for, isn't it?"

Orrin squatted on his haunches with a contented half-smile on his lips. His eyes seemed to look through McFarland to a point somewhere deep inside the mountains. His dark hair was in disarray. "I'm not here to hurt you. They sent me here to reason with you. They want you to join them, to stop opposing them. They want to help Wellington, they really do. They'll share their technology with us freely if you just stop trying to turn everyone against them."

"Oh. come on," said McFarland bitterly. "What makes you think they'll keep their word even then? They're just going to turn us all into zombies anyway. Why give us anything? In the end they'll have everything they want, we'll all end up their slaves, and three quarters of the people in this town will shout 'Hallelujah!' while it happens."

"Will that be so bad, Carl? Honestly?"

McFarland's bloody, cracked lips narrowed. "I don't know," he said. "You tell me."

"Carl—"

But McFarland just shook his head, the tears starting up again. "Oh, dammit, Orrin, how did this ever happen to you, anyway?"

The idiotic half-smile wavered a bit.

"Please, Orrin. We used to be friends."

Orrin released a long, slow breath after a moment, and sat down in the grass. He wrapped his arms around his knees. "Once the revival was under way and you were inside the tent, I couldn't see any activity at all out in the wagon. Earlier there'd been a lot, so now I figured everyone was helping with the revival. I thought I'd just go poke around a little and see what I could see. There were no lights on."

"You dope," said McFarland. "They can see in infrared."

Orrin nodded. "I know that now, of course. If you'd told me a little more of what you knew yesterday, though, I might not have been so incautious."

That stung, even though it was delivered in a matter-of-fact tone of voice. "Dammit, Orrin, I told you just to watch! I didn't want you out—"

Orrin held up a hand, palm out. "Carl, please. I didn't mean that as a recrimination. It's simply a fact. You should have known how much a teenage boy would have wanted to be a hero—especially one that had admired *you* so much for so long."

"I'm no hero," said McFarland softly. Orrin said nothing, and it suddenly registered on McFarland that the boy had referred to himself in the past tense. McFarland clenched shut his eyes. Every time I turn around, he thought, I've murdered someone different.

Birds sang.

"Listen, Orrin," said McFarland suddenly, wiping his face, "what's going to happen is going to happen. Can you forget all that for a few minutes and do something for me? A favor?"

"What favor?"

McFarland wiped his hands on his torn pants. His white, blue-veined legs showed through the holes. "Play a hand of gin with me. It's probably the last chance we'll ever have . . . and I already miss having someone good to play against. Hell, having anybody at *all*."

Orrin considered this. "One hand?"

McFarland nodded.

"All right. But I'll fetch the cards."

"That's fine," said McFarland. "You know where I keep them."

While Orrin was inside, McFarland scooted himself around in the grass until he was facing the house, his back to the overlook. Orrin returned after a minute or two with a pack of bent, torn, and faded Bicycle cards held delicately in his hand. He sat down in the grass opposite McFarland. "One hand," he said, a stern reminder.

McFarland nodded, and Orrin dealt.

Since his left hand wouldn't close, McFarland had to hold his ten cards in his right hand, then awkwardly draw and discard with two fingers of his left. Every breath hurt his chest, and he nearly dropped his cards twice when he leaned over the discard pile and the broken edge of a rib tore into the muscles of his chest. After a few plays, McFarland held a king, a jack, two tens, and assorted lower cards of differing suits. A very bad hand. "I suppose they've changed your magic words," said McFarland, pretending to study his cards.

Orrin drew a card from the stock, fitted it into his hand, then discarded a jack. His open, unfocused gaze seemed to take in his cards, McFarland, and everything else in the landscape all at one time. "What do you mean?" he said.

"Of course they did," said McFarland, half to himself. "They wouldn't have sent you up here alone otherwise."

Orrin set down his cards. "What are you talking about, Carl?" His maddening half-smile never changed.

McFarland flicked an ant off the discard pile. He let out a deep, painful breath. "There are two keywords that the nanomachines in and around your auditory nerve are programmed to recognize," he said. "You *did* realize that nanomachines are what brought you back from the dead, didn't you?"

Orrin nodded, clearly impatient.

"Okay, then." It hurt to speak, and McFarland could hear the strain in his own voice. "The first keyword causes a signal to be sent to the nanomachines in your brain, damping the neural activity in your prefrontal lobe. Now, the prefrontal lobe is more or less where your will is centered, so when this happens, you've pretty much become a slave to the voice that spoke the keyword. Your will is no longer your own. You'll do anything you're told. But then when you hear the second keyword, the damper is released." McFarland looked up. "Do you follow all that?"

"Yes, I follow it," said Orrin, picking up his cards again. "It's your draw."

McFarland picked up the jack from the discard pile. As he tried fitting it into his hand, he dropped half his cards into the grass. "Damn," he muttered, and began picking them up. "But anyway, Orrin, while you're in your little trance, your master or whatever can instruct you to respond in the same way to a different pair of keywords and to forget the original ones." He paused for a moment, as if to consider what he was saying. "Well, I suppose it's actually the nanomachines he's reprogramming, not you . . . but that's just splitting hairs." He fit the last card back into his hand. "Okay, go ahead."

"You still have to discard," said Orrin evenly, but his smile was beginning to seem a little forced. "And if you're suggesting that I'm only trying to convince you to stop opposing us because I'm in some kind of hypnotic trance, then you're wrong. I'm here because I was asked to come, and because I believe in what I'm telling you."

McFarland threw down his king. "I don't doubt that for a second, Orrin. I'd be able to tell if you were in a trance. And anyway, a subject in a trance can't be trusted to carry out a series of complex tasks away from its master. When you damp the will, you also reduce the attention span, and the subject is too easily distracted to get anything accomplished. That's one problem we never got around. Of course, even subjects *not* in trances are still fairly suggestible . . ."

Orrin had picked up the king, and now he discarded a queen. "I know what you're trying to do, Carl," he said, "and you're not distracting me from anything, not even with this pointless game of cards. I chose to play with you out of respect for our former friendship, not because I was helpless to tell you no, as you seem to be suggesting."

"I'm not suggesting *anything*, you moron," said McFarland, a bit huffily. "I'm just trying to help you a little. You *know* I've always believed that the better you understand your situation, the better you'll be able to cope with it. I've *always* tried to teach you that."

"*You* should understand *your* situation," said Orrin, setting his cards down again. "Pastor Smith knows who you are. He's seen your name on documents related to this Project Rapture you were a part of. He can't let you slip away unconverted. You'll be one of us, one way or another."

McFarland's hands were trembling as he drew a fresh card from the stock. He had never mentioned Project Rapture to Orrin; this wasn't a bluff. No doubt the preacher had been ready for what McFarland had pulled at the previous night's revival. He had fed McFarland just enough rope to hang himself with . . .

Orrin was right. They certainly wouldn't risk leaving him around as a loose end.

McFarland had drawn an ace, but it didn't help his hand any. Watching Orrin over his cards, he said casually, "You haven't happened to have run into Rachel out there in Goonland, have you?"

"Why?" said Orrin, his smile faltering. "Has s-s-s—?" His face seemed to ripple like a horse's flank shivering away flies, and then it settled back into its beatific mask. "Has something happened to her?"

"She's dead," McFarland said angrily. He slapped a seven down on the discard pile and winced at the pain that shot through his hand. "Your friends killed *her*, too, and after I brought her back to life they killed her again. Maybe they've revived her *again* by now. I don't know. Probably."

Orrin's face remained very still. "It would be . . . gratifying," he said in a soft voice, "to find that Rachel has joined our cause."

"*Bullshit!*" spat McFarland. "You're feeding yourself a big line of it, and you know it." He pushed himself to his feet, ignoring the pain in his hand and chest. "I'm going to have a glass of milk. Do you want one?"

Orrin picked up the seven, discarded a ten, and laid down his hand. "Gin," he said, then looked up. He was no longer smiling, and his hands twitched as if they didn't know quite what to do. "That's a tradition of ours, isn't it? Gin and milk."

McFarland would have laughed if he hadn't been so full of rage and grief. Instead he walked around Orrin headed up to the house, limping from an injury he hadn't noticed before. "I'll be right back."

His house was cold inside. His nose had begun to run, so he wiped it on a dishtowel in the kitchen. He pulled open a drawer beside the sink, but then he paused for a moment, catching a glimpse of his faint reflection in the window that looked out on the backyard. He moved closer to the window. He resembled a ghost—perhaps Marley's ghost from *A Christmas Carol*—bruised and bloody, pale and transparent, with two blackened eyes and a cruelly ruined nose. His reflection overlaid the wind turbines that marched up the mountain behind the house, and watching them turn he thought about all he given to Wellington—the turbines that generated their electricity, the heaters and pumps that kept their moat circulating in winter, the water tanks that let them gather food from the lethal desert, and everything else.

It didn't come close to making up for the lives he had allowed to be lost.

From the drawer he took an old and rusted carving knife. He

hurried to the front door before any other ghosts could rise up and stop him.

Orrin was still sitting on the grass where McFarland had left him, his back to the house. He was shuffling through the deck of cards, examining them as if they concealed some cryptic message. McFarland walked up behind him, then set his left hand gently on Orrin's head. Orrin set down the cards. "The others won't let you get away, Carl," he said.

"That's a moot point," said McFarland. "I don't want to get away. I want to stop them."

"You can't."

"I can try." McFarland blinked his suddenly stinging eyes. "I can be at their damn revival tonight and try."

"The only way you'll get anywhere near that tent tonight is if they carry you in dead, Carl."

McFarland felt a chill march up his spine, like a troop of tiny soldiers in boots of ice. "I know," he said softly. "I know."

He looked out at the silvery desert for what seemed like eons, felt the wind against his back, smelled the tang of the fir trees. He closed his eyes and breathed deeply. "Is this the way you want to live, Orrin? Really? All you have to do is say the word, you know."

Orrin shuddered and opened his mouth, but only a breathy squeak came out. He opened his mouth again, and in a small voice said, "No."

And as McFarland set the tip of the knife against Orrin's back, just to the left of the spine, he saw his father's fist smashing down on the pulpit of the old downtown church, heard that deep, rich voice declaring, "But even so, my brothers and sisters, there are some sins that even the redeeming blood of Christ cannot cleanse from our souls, sins for which we must pay with our very *lives* if we are ever to see the kingdom of God!"

Tears streamed down McFarland's cheeks. "Oh, God, Orrin, I wish you'd killed me when you had the chance," he whispered, and then he leaned all his weight on the handle of the knife.

7

McFARLAND CAME IN FROM THE FRONT YARD WITH DIRT GROUND into the knees of his overalls and dried blood all the way from his hands to his elbows. He had tried to wipe his hands clean on the grass, but it hadn't done any good. He had managed to get Orrin's head buried in the old flower garden out back, but with his hand and his ribs they way they were, he had been able to do little more in front than spade a shallow mound of dirt over the rest of the body. There was no chance now that Orrin could be revived a second time.

He promised himself that if he ever saw Rachel alive again, he would do the same for her.

McFarland wanted to rest, but he couldn't let himself. It was just past noon, and people would be starting to file home from the morning Easter services. He could think of only one way to prevent what was going to happen to them all that night, but if he allowed himself to rest, gave himself a chance to think about it, he knew he could never go through with it. He would die a coward and a murderer, with all his sins still on his head.

He went to the living room and pulled an old King James Bible down from one of the bookcases. It was only one Bible

among many, but this was the one Pastor McFarland had referred to most while preparing his sermons, an edition put out by
the Latter-day Saints. His father had never held with any doctrine preached by the Mormons, but he always said their Bible
had the best damn index anyone had ever put together.

Without that index, McFarland knew he wouldn't get anywhere.

He took the Bible to the kitchen table. The passages he was
looking for were somewhere in the Gospels; he knew that much.
He closed his eyes, let his mind drift back to his father's sermons,
dredged up phrases and portions of phrases from the deepest
parts of his memory. He looked up the most prominent words
from those phrases in the index, and after about twenty minutes
of false leads he had found the passages he wanted.

He marked the verses in St. Matthew by folding down the
corner of the page, and then for the next hour he concentrated
on memorizing the verses from St. Mark. These were the most
important. He repeated them over and over, first with the Bible
open and then with it closed. When he felt confident enough, he
stood up and limped from room to room, repeating the passage
as he walked, until he could do it without even thinking. He
took a five-minute break on the porch, then stood up and recited
the verses again, word for word.

He tackled the passage from St. Matthew the same way, and
when he could recite that one without effort, he repeated them
both, one after another, for another half-hour.

The sun trickled slowly west. At around three, McFarland
packed the Bible and an open package of manna into his cloth
grocery bag and headed down from the ridge, reciting scripture
as he went. He didn't look back, even though he knew he might
never see his home again. "No man," as he had read in St. Luke,

chasing down one of his false leads, "having put his hand to the plough, and looking back, is fit for the kingdom of God."

If he wanted to pull this off, he had to take his scriptures seriously.

Near the edge of town, where the overgrown path from the ridge first widened out into a street, an even narrower trail angled off into the trees to the southwest. Across from this trailhead, tucked in among the aspens and cottonwoods, its driveway abutting on the beginnings of the street, was the Wellington Fire District Station No. 1, which housed the town's only two remaining electric vehicles—a small fire engine and a larger hook-and-ladder. They were more often used to wash away plague than to fight actual fires. Denny Merrifield, the fire chief, sat out front on a battered packing crate beside the high garage door. When Merrifield spotted McFarland, he ran to the side of the driveway and scooped up a rock. "Hey, you better stay outta town, old man!" he yelled. "I don't think you're welcome here!" He hurled the rock, then went back to his seat, laughing, when McFarland instinctively ducked. The rock sailed wide, but McFarland's stomach was clenched in fear nonetheless, and the sharp, stabbing pain in his chest had returned. Merrifield had been part of Jed Thomas's gang the night before.

Breathing harshly, he turned down the southwesterly trail, swinging his bag at his side, still reciting his Bible verses, and trying not to look over his shoulder. "That's a good place for you!" called out Merrifield's distant voice. "You two nuts can just shack up together and leave the rest of us the hell alone!"

McFarland would have to enter town a different way when he finished with this little side trip. Surely Christ's admonition to offer the left cheek to whomever had smitten you on the right did not apply to the current situation. Even in religion, there was room for a liberal dose of common sense.

Limpid sunlight filtered down to the forest floor in shifting patches, and branches rustled overhead like whispering ghosts. McFarland shivered and tried to limp more quickly. After about a hundred and fifty yards, he came to a clearing which contained a small log house and a shed. Rusted scraps of machinery littered the ground all around the house, and two mangy yellow dogs slept in a big pool of sunlight.

Fuzzy Rutledge lived here, in the house his father Bucky Rutledge had built. Bucky had been a jack-of-all-trades—handyman, gardener, woodsman, tinker, herbalist—but most importantly, he had inherited a small silver concession southeast of Walker Lake, which he worked himself. Not trusting anyone else with his ore, he had brought it home and processed it himself as well, in the shed behind the house. McFarland was betting that Fuzzy hadn't thrown anything out in the twenty-two years his pap had been dead, including Bucky's ore-processing chemicals.

If the yard was any indication, it was a safe bet.

As McFarland threaded a path between cannibalized drill presses and shattered car engines, one of the dogs lifted its head and whined. Once upon a time, McFarland had known the dogs that lived here well; he had come here often to get parts from Bucky for his turbines and transformers and the like. But McFarland hadn't stopped in here for years. Fuzzy liked to keep to himself even more than his father had, and people were more than happy to let him. He did his time on the perimeter and helped with things around town like everyone else, but as soon as he was finished he came straight back home to tinker with his strange machines that never seemed to actually do anything.

Fuzzy poked his head around the corner of the house. "Who

is it?" he said gruffly. He was a small, wiry man in his mid-forties; his eyes were dark and lively, and a thin layer of black stubble covered his scalp, cheeks, chin, and jaw, going grizzled at the edges. He had kept his hair that way since he was a child. His dark eyes widened when he caught sight of McFarland. "Jesus God above, what the hell kinda creature are you?"

McFarland spread his arms. "It's just me, Fuzzy. Carl McFarland."

Fuzzy stepped out from behind the house in a sort of a half-crouch, moving sideways, constantly shifting from one foot to the other as if he were treading on hot coals. He squinted at McFarland from several feet away; his eyes were going bad from all the close work he did, and he refused to wear glasses. "Jeez, Carl, you look like hell," he said. "For a second there, I thought you were the Devil himself, come to drag me away." Then Fuzzy went pale and took a few steps back. "Wait a minute, wait a minute. People in town been tellin' me maybe you *are* the Devil. Been raisin' people from the dead and stuff like that."

"Oh, calm down," said McFarland, waving his free hand dismissively. "I'm not the Devil, and you shouldn't believe everything you hear in town, anyway."

Fuzzy took a couple of dancing steps forward. "Are you sure? I mean, you look all red an' all . . ."

Exasperated, McFarland dropped his cloth bag and thrust out his hands. His broken rib ground into muscle, and he clenched his teeth. "Look, Fuzzy, it's just blood—*blood*. Jed Thomas and a bunch of his boys beat me up last night, and I haven't really had a chance to clean up. They broke my nose and my hand and a couple of ribs and who the hell knows what else!"

Fuzzy's hands went up as if he expected to be hit. "Okay, okay, I believe you, I do. Jeez." He ran a hand over the stubble of his hair and shrugged his shoulders as if he were working out a crick in his neck. "You don't have to get all sore like that."

"I apologize," said McFarland, wincing as the rib stabbed him again. "It's been kind of a bad day. I didn't mean to snap at you."

Fuzzy smoothed his woolen shirt and looked off into the woods as if he refused to be mollified.

McFarland coughed suddenly, painfully, and the breath whistled through his teeth. "Listen, I'm in a bit of a hurry here," he said, feeling himself begin to sway on his feet. "I came to see if I could borrow something of your daddy's that might be in his shed."

Fuzzy cocked his head to one side and regarded McFarland with suspicion. "And what might that be?"

"A jar, a canister, a tin—*something*—filled with a granular white powder and with the letters KCN printed on the side."

"And assuming I *have* such a thing," said Fuzzy, tilting his head from side to side with the cadence of the sentence, "why should I give it to *you?*"

"Your daddy always shared with me, Fuzzy." McFarland coughed again and tried not to let himself sound angry. "And I only need a little bit of it."

"Well, the way I see it, you're not the most popular fellah in town at the moment. What happens if ol' Jed finds out I've been helping you, and he and his boys decide to come give *me* a little hell?"

"Believe me, if anyone finds out you gave me this stuff, they'll call you a hero." No matter *how* things turn out, McFarland added to himself.

"But what if—"

McFarland had had enough. "Dammit, Fuzzy, I don't want to hear any more buts! Maybe I really am the Devil, and maybe I'm going to burn your whole spread here to the ground and then suck your eyeballs out with a straw if you don't get me that goddamn powder!"

Fuzzy hesitated for a moment, a stunned look on his face, then made a beeline for the shed. The dogs looked up as he passed, but did not move or try to follow. McFarland starting coughing and couldn't stop, and his chest felt as if it were ripping apart from the inside. Something warm and coppery landed in his mouth, and he spat it on the ground. A gobbet of bloody tissue.

"Wonderful," he muttered. "Just wonderful."

After a minute or two, Fuzzy returned from the shed bearing a large, mint-green plastic jar. The letters KCN had been scrawled on the side with a black felt marker, though the writing had faded to brownish gray. A crude skull and crossbones had been drawn beneath the letters. "Is this what you're lookin' for?"

McFarland wiped flecks of blood from his lips, then took the proffered jar. When he unscrewed the lid, he caught a faint almondlike odor. The substance inside looked pretty much like salt. For the first time that day, McFarland smiled. Potassium cyanide. The answer to all his problems. In dilute solution, the granular powder formed ions that would draw the silver out of finely divided ore. The silver could then be recovered by reducing the solution with zinc dust.

But that was hardly the property that interested McFarland.

He sat down carefully on the ground, then reached into his cloth bag and pulled out a small chunk of manna. The manna was white, and it had the consistency of medium-soft cheese. He formed a ball of the stuff with about the diameter of U.S. quarter, then pressed the tip of his finger into the ball. There was a small scoop inside the jar, and McFarland used it to fill the hollow space halfway with potassium cyanide. It was awkward holding the ball with the fingers of his broken hand, but he managed not to spill any of the powder outside the hollow space.

"Hey, hey," said Fuzzy, who was watching this all with fascination, "you know that stuff there's poison, don't you?"

"Yes, I know," said McFarland. He pinched the hollow space shut, then rolled the ball a little to smooth out the surface. "That's the whole point."

Fuzzy nodded sagely. "Hey, Carl, what does that mean there, anyway—KCN?"

McFarland figured that the less Fuzzy was able to tell anybody, the better off they both would be. "It stands for the, uh— the Knights of Columbus . . . of Nevada. Your daddy used to do some fix-it work around their old meeting hall." With the poisoned ball of manna held protectively in his right hand, McFarland stood up. He coughed again. "I appreciate this, Fuzzy. I really do. Anytime you need anything of mine, it's yours."

A sly look came into Fuzzy's eyes. "How's about that Bible there in your bag?"

McFarland was looking at the bag, wondering how he would pick it up in his left hand. "What Bible?"

Fuzzy stamped his foot. "Oh, come on, Carl! My pap didn't raise no idiots! I saw it when you were gettin' out that manna! I'm startin' to think maybe it's time I got a little religion for myself, what with all the crazy talk over in town. Maybe if the Devil really does come for me, this'll keep him away. Now, can I have it, or do I have to go shootin' off my mouth how you're fixin' to poison someone?"

"Hell, Fuzzy, take it." McFarland had wanted to study his verses again on the way into town, but he was worried about dropping or crushing the manna-ball with his ungainly hands if he tried to hold the Bible open and read and walk through the forest all at the same time. "Keep the whole damn bag, in fact. You're welcome to it."

A bright smile lit Fuzzy's face. "Thanks, Carl! My pap always said you were a miracle sent us from God! I shouldn't never have disbelieved him!" He scooped up the bag and capered back around the corner of his house. "God bless you, Carl! God bless you!"

"Yeah, right," said McFarland to himself. He limped out of the clearing with what felt like a burning spear piercing his chest.

8

"Every kingdom divided against . . . against itself is brought to desolation," recited McFarland as he rounded the corner of Winnemucca Street. He was breathing as if he had just run a marathon, and he had coughed up more bloody chunks of tissue along the way. His chest felt as if someone were performing open-heart surgery on him without the benefit of anesthetic, but he thought it was probably that very pain that had kept him clear-headed enough to be able to walk so far.

And it was only a little bit farther.

He had emerged from the woods four blocks back. Fortunately no one had seen him—or if any people had, they had been too frightened by McFarland's appearance to do or say anything about it.

He rolled the little ball of manna between his fingers like a worry bead, feeling it, smoothing it out, letting it reassure him as he recited his scriptures. His limp was getting worse; he figured he had probably started out from home with a slight sprain, but now his right ankle was swollen and tender. It wouldn't matter much longer, though.

The sun was sinking, casting long shadows across the street, and the sky glowed a rich dark blue. Candles began to burn behind dark window panes in the houses around him. The revival wouldn't start until after sundown. Still plenty of time.

Only a few doors more . . .

He turned up the path to the Burlingames' house. He could see candlelight flickering inside, and he heard the murmur of low conversation. A cool breeze stirred his hair.

A queer sensation gripped his belly, and his hands and feet suddenly felt as if they were made of ice. There was still time to turn around, to leave . . .

No, he told himself. Remember why you're here. Remember who you are. Remember your new name.

Panic flooded him. What if I *can't* remember? What if it doesn't work? Oh, God . . .

Get a grip! *Orrin* remembered, and he didn't know what he was in for. You do.

Now do it.

McFarland tipped his head back and tried to relax. Pain screamed from his chest, but he ignored it. He repeated his key phrase over and over in his mind, like a mantra, until it was fixed there solidly, until it repeated itself automatically without any conscious effort.

Then he knocked on the door.

The conversation stopped, and he heard the sound of a chair scraping back along the floor. Footsteps approached. McFarland waited until he could see June Burlingame's dark silhouette through the screen, then he popped the manna-ball into his mouth.

"Yes, who is it?" she said as she emerged into the half-light of the approaching dusk, taking on form and color. Her simple woolen dress was pressed and fresh, and her face looked pinched, as if she had been eating grapefruit.

When her eyes took in McFarland's blood-encrusted face and outstretched bloody hands, her mouth opened in the beginnings of a scream.

For my sins, McFarland thought, and he bit down on the manna-ball.

Poisoned saliva ran down his throat, and a great convulsive pain racked him as cells all throughout his body lost their ability to metabolize oxygen from the blood.

He fell toward the screen door as June Burlingame screamed, and felt nothing more.

Blackness. Timelessness. Nothingness. A universe without form, and void.

No cause. No effect.

Nothing.

And then, shooting into the void, a thin thread of silver light—

10

IMPERATIVE! **DECLARED THE SILVER LIGHT, ILLUMINATING THE** darkness. *Organization!*

Offshoots branched away from the thin line of light in every direction, and more offshoots branched away from those. A structure took shape, bilaterally symmetrical, and lines of feedback looped back from the extremities to report.

The central silver light received this feedback, and found it good.

Imperative! it declared again. *Replication!*

The command flashed away down branching silver lines. The structure vibrated at the sound, and its lines thickened. Vibrations raced to the extremities, then raced back, and the structure thickened again, and again.

The reports flashed in, and again they were all good.

Imperative! Integration!

As the command echoed back from every terminus of the network of silver lines, it trailed behind it slim filaments of red. This red subnetwork linked Thoracic Sector, Tarsal Sector Dexter, Metacarpal Sector Sinister, and Maxillofacial Sector to the central silver light, and as the original impulses were reflected back out into the structural network, the filaments of red were smoothed away.

The impulses returned, and the reports they brought were good.

Imperative! Initialization!

The command streaked off, and the reports filtered back quickly. All was in readiness; all was prepared.

All was good.

The silver light rested, waiting.

11

Memory overseers herded the electrochemical impulse endlessly through its appointed cycle of neurons, bound it tightly in place, never letting it escape. *Legion, Legion, Legion, Legion . . .*

They penned it in, firmly—until the coming of the final command:

"Awake, o thou that sleepest, and *arise!*"

12

McFarland blinked, then opened his eyes.

The light blinded him at first, but filters damped it down until his vision was a bearable mosaic of discrete white pixels. The hot, moist air colliding with his skin registered not exactly as a sensation, but in a more abstract manner, as if he were reading the temperature and relative humidity from a pair of scales.

He felt random thoughts flashing through his mind on parallel paths:

```
{CurrentSituation} = DEATH ?
[{CurrentSelf} = OLDSELF] ∨ [{CurrentSelf} =
NEWSELF] ?
SPIRIT ∈ {CurrentSelf} ?
[SPIRIT ∪ {CurrentSelf}] = SOUL ?
NEWSELF > OLDSELF ?
```

But the thoughts raced away when he consciously tried to seize hold of them, to be processed by other, more capable mental threads.

A dark patch intruded on the left edge of the mosaic. Mc-

Farland found that he could shift the field of his vision without turning his head, as if he were adjusting the focal point of a wide-angle lens. The dark patch spread until it dominated the center of the mosaic, then resolved into the form of a man.

The preacher.

McFarland felt joy, but it was the sort of joy that comes from fitting a problematic piece into a jigsaw puzzle, or from finding clean roots to a complicated nth-order polynomial. It was an intellectual joy, but it was as yet incomplete.

A flesh-colored object loomed before McFarland's eyes. A hand. McFarland raised his own hand, and felt his motor cortex calculating the angle and velocity through which his arm must move in order to grasp the preacher's hand. Then there was contact—a complex system of tactile feedback arranged as surfaces in a three-dimensional textural array.

He pushed the figures and charts to the back of his mind, and let the preacher help him to his feet. He could detect no feedback from his body's nocireceptors; he was healed, and free of pain.

"And now we see, my beloved brothers and sisters," cried the preacher—in a voice McFarland tried not to hear as jags and valleys plotted against a frequency graph—"that the loving, forgiving hand of the Lord Jesus Christ is extended to *all* mankind, if only they will *grasp* it! It is extended even unto the vilest of sinners, if they will but repent, and forsake their sinful ways!"

There was an explosion of white noise—cheering, applause, and hallelujahs.

He saw the crowd as a pointillistic expanse of varied colors and shades. His eyes damped down the lights by another few increments, and his vision shifted back and forth across the platform. Beyond the preacher, at the far extent of what he could see, was a shape he recognized as Adolf. Besides two other churchies he didn't recognize off to his right, they were alone on the platform before the crowd.

Good. His had been the first dead body resurrected this Easter evening. It had been a plum too great for the preacher to resist.

McFarland felt the joy of another puzzle piece snapping neatly into place.

And he could feel a pressure building up in his speech queue.

The preacher clapped McFarland on the back and cried out to the crowd, "And as you have witnessed here this evening, even *this* man, this former lieutenant in the armies of darkness, can be redeemed from sin, can feel the overwhelming weight of God's hand strike him down to the earth—and then raise him up again with his garments cleansed from the blood of this world!"

The compulsion to speak was nearly to great to resist, but McFarland held his tongue.

The preacher turned to him. "Friend, can you tell us your name, now that you've returned to us from the land beyond the grave?"

McFarland opened the floodgates of his voice box a tiny bit. "My name . . . ?"

The preacher nodded. "Yes, brother." Bright pinpricks of reflected light glinted from his eyes.

McFarland smiled. The floodgates opened wide as he addressed the crowd:

"My name is Legion, for we are many!"

He heard the wondering gasps of indrawn breath from all throughout the tent.

The preacher laughed, but McFarland detected a heightened gleam from the man's sweaty forehead. Infrared analysis told him the preacher's skin temperature had dropped suddenly with the outpouring of perspiration. "Surely you're playing a joke on us, my good—"

McFarland pushed the preacher's arm away roughly. "I do not *joke!*" he said, modulating his voice into a low, fierce growl, lower than he could have spoken before dying and being reawakened. "We are the same of whom St. Mark wrote, who possessed the body of a man in the country of the Gadarenes, who had his dwelling among the tombs; and no man could bind him—no, not with chains—and neither could any man tame him. And always, night and day, he was in the mountains, and in the tombs, crying, and cutting himself with stones."

The preacher stumbled back a step at the force in McFarland's voice, his face blanching in terror. No one made a sound in the giant revival tent; the weight of the silence was like an oppressive fist.

McFarland turned to the audience, gesturing as he had seen the preacher do, and smiling a feral smile. "But when we saw Jesus afar off," he said in his unnatural growl, "we ran and worshipped him, and cried with a loud voice, and said, 'What have we to do with thee, Jesus, thou Son of the most high God? I adjure thee by God that thou torment me not.'

"And he said unto us, 'Come out of the man, thou unclean spirit.'"

He pointed a finger at the shaken preacher. "If thou art a man of God, do even as Jesus before thee hast done! Cast us out from this body, and command us to *depart!* Cast us into a herd of goats, even as Jesus allowed us to enter into a herd of swine, that we might not relinquish our hold on bodies of flesh!" His face twisted into an angry snarl. "O thou child of hell, *we defy thee to cast us out!*"

No one seemed to breathe.

The preacher, though pale, stood up straight. He slowly raised one arm behind his head, as if preparing to fence, and then pointed the other at McFarland. "Unclean spirit—or spirits, as that may be," he said, voice gathering strength as he spoke, "I command you in the name of that same Jesus Christ whom I serve, and before whom you bow, to come out of this body and *depart!*"

And below his breath, where only McFarland could hear, he hissed, "*Montezuma!*"

No experimental subject McFarland had ever worked with in the course of Project Rapture had ever been expecting to return from the dead. This was one of the important factors in the zombies' vulnerability to mind control. It was a theoretical bug in the system—but one that, since it had never been encountered, had never been ironed out. The subjects were confused upon reawakening, disoriented, and never recovered complete equilibrium, making them more amenable to the surrender of will.

McFarland, on the other hand, had known exactly what was coming, and he thought he had at least an even chance of resisting the keyword—but even so, at the preacher's command he felt his will battered by an almost overwhelming authoritarian force. He felt tiny bits of himself rushing into the prefrontal lobe to help shore up the crumbling structure of his will. The retaining wall held, at least for the moment, and McFarland's face froze as he poured every ounce of effort he could muster into pushing back at the force pressing in against him.

The command word coruscated with awful, seductive power, and the wall trembled. Not for me, McFarland thought desperately. For Rachel and Orrin, for Eileen and Hillary, for Dale Fenton Bradley and James Ivie and Fuzzy Rutledge and everyone else who had lost anything to nanotechnology or *would* lose it if he failed . . .

He felt something yield in his brain, like the slow tearing of cheesecloth—

—and the attacking force broke up, like surf crashing back into the sea after slamming against a cliff of solid rock.

He could sense a great rent in the fabric of his mind, but a quick mental inventory told him what had been lost: the traitorous parts of himself that could damp his own will. The reconstructive nanomachines in his brain, sensing hurt, pain, injury, had destroyed them, like white blood cells attacking an invading infection.

The penultimate piece of the puzzle snapped satisfyingly into place.

"And now thou seest that thou canst not cast us out," he said in a soft, menacing voice, into which he let seep none of his joy.

The preacher stumbled backward, eyes wide, and fell over on his backside when his heel caught on a crack between the planks of the platform. "But—but—"

McFarland stood over him, shoulders hunched like a strangler's. Adolf and the others moved in, but it was clear they had no idea what to do. They looked back and forth between McFarland and the preacher in confusion. "And why canst thou not cast us out?" said McFarland. "For thou art an agent of that same Devil who rules *us*, and all thy miracles have been performed by his power. As Jesus declared unto our brothers the Pharisees, 'Every kingdom divided against itself is brought to desolation, and every city or house divided against itself shall not stand. And if Satan cast out Satan, he is divided against himself. How shall then his kingdom stand? And if I by Beelzebub cast out devils, by whom do your children cast them out?

"'Therefore, they shall be your *judges.*'"

McFarland turned again to the audience, pointing a stiff and accusatory arm at the preacher, who trembled, sweating, at his feet. "It is said that the Devil will not support his children at the last day. These men have attempted to enslave you with their false doctrines. They have tried to steal away your children, and tried to steal your very souls. Judge them as you will."

He turned and walked to the rear of the platform, then descended the rollaway stairs. He heard a great roar as the crowd surged to its feet, shouting in riotous anger, and he heard the preacher screaming, *"Alpha! Alpha! Stop them! Hold them back, you idiots! Hold them back!"*

Alpha, thought McFarland. So *that* was the new keyword. The other one was probably "Omega." The first and the last. The beginning and the ending. Appropriate. Very appropriate. And it might just come in handy to know.

He dropped to his knees and crawled beneath the edge of the tent.

13

HE EMERGED INTO A CLEAR, COOL NIGHT. HE STOOD, STRETCH-ing muscles that felt more responsive than they had felt in decades. He savored the sensation, the intricate interplay of the electrical impulses and chemical reactions that allowed him to walk, to breathe, to keep his balance, to think. He filtered out the sounds of carnage from the tent behind him. The night breezes moved across his skin in delicious sensuality.

He crossed the empty field to the edge of the moat, where he had left his water tank the night before. Beyond the moat, a waning moon silvered the desert with its thin light. In the distance stood one lone wagon, beaming a silent lullaby to the surrounding landscape.

McFarland clambered down into the moat, refilled his tank, and then strapped it on. As he climbed up the far bank, into the desert, the final piece of the puzzle fell into place.

All throughout his previous life, he had been wrong in the way he tried to teach science. There was a more effective way of expressing his beliefs, of converting his students to the doctrines he considered truth.

McFarland headed for the wagon, laying plans for his new religion. He would preach physics, and physics would set his people free.

www.ingramcontent.com/pod-product-compliance
Lightning Source LLC
Chambersburg PA
CBHW020149180626
46810CB00004B/1805